Jane Schaffer

Illustrated by
John Lightbourne and Geraldine Mitchell

Seven Arches
Publishing

Published in March 2010
By Seven Arches Publishing
27, Church Street, Nassington, Peterborough PE8 61QG
www.sevenarchespublishing.co.uk

Cover design by John Bigwood and Alan McGlynn
Book Design by Alan McGlynn

Printed in Great Britain by imprintdigital.net

ISBN 978-0-9556169-6-9

To Margaret Davies
whose historical knowledge and story ideas were
invaluable in the writing of this book.

<IF THIS IS THE FIRST TIME YOU HAVE READ ONE
OF THE BOOKS THAT RECORDS THE ADVENTURES
OF DANNY HIGGINS IN A TIME ZONE DIFFERENT TO
TODAY, YOU NEED TO KNOW>

> That SHARP stands for The Scientific History and Art Reclamation Programme.

> That time slip is something that you might suffer if you travel through time and space, in a similar way to how you get jet lag when you fly long distances on a jet air liner.

> That if you travel through time and space you are a xrosmonaut.

CHAPTER 1

An Aunt In Lichfield

'News!' exclaimed his mum excitedly as Danny came in through the back door, banging the ton of books that was in his school bag, down on the floor.

Mrs Higgins was sitting at the kitchen table reading the second page of a neatly written three-page letter. Danny was amazed how many people his mother knew, who still wrote letters. It all added to Danny's conviction that the Higgins household, together with their friends and relatives, were about fifty years behind the times. The next thing his mother said, explained completely why the communication was a letter and not an e-mail. The letter came from his seventy-year-old great aunt.

'Aunt Mabel has invited us to go and stay for a few days. She says here she'd love to have us all come over at half-term if we haven't arranged anything.'

Yes well, thought Danny, that's about as exciting as the geography lesson I've just had.

'Oh great, I love it at Aunt Mabel's – she's the best aunt ever!' exclaimed Jenny, Danny's eight-year-old sister. Danny rated Aunt Mabel as well but he wasn't going to say so. Instead he went over to the fridge, poured himself a glass of orange juice and said:

'Well aren't we the lucky ones?'

'Danny!' said Mrs Higgins in a shocked voice.

'Well, I mean – Mark gets to go to America for two weeks, one of which is in school time, and we get four days in Lichfield!'

'Danny, you know very well you like Aunt Mabel,' said his mum reproachfully.

'We always have fun with her,' said Jenny. 'She cooks the best meals ever. She takes us to absolutely great places, like, like you know that safari park where I fell over that time and grazed my knees badly and she does midnight feasts and things…and…' Jenny's defence of Aunt Mabel was coming to a stuttering halt because Danny was giving her one of his well-prac- tised "so what" looks. She hadn't quite got over the fact that her thirteen-year-old brother was a secondary kid now and secondary kids don't get excited about driving forty miles to visit aunts.

After Danny had made himself some toast with the extra seeded, extra nutritious, extra brown bread that Mrs Higgins always bought, he went upstairs and banged his bedroom door. Mrs Higgins said nothing but raised her eyebrows and sighed a little. Danny had always been such a thoughtful child. Jenny got back to the drawing she'd been doing before Danny came in but she looked a bit dejected.

'Don't worry Jenny. He'll enjoy it once we're there. Aunt Mabel will win him round, you'll see.'

'And Rocket,' said Jenny. 'How can he have forgotten about Rocket?' Rocket, Aunt Mabel's dog was loved by Jenny almost as much as its owner.

'He hasn't Jenny. It's just an act he's putting on. You know he wouldn't be human if he wasn't a bit jealous of Mark. His parents have so much money – they can buy Mark anything he wants, and they do. And now taking him off to America during school time, well it's just irresponsible.' Mrs Higgins shook her head.

Danny threw himself down on his bed, kicked off his school shoes and, in between munching mouthfuls of toast, reached for his DS. But he didn't start it up straight away. He was feeling mean. He knew his mum was very fond of Aunt Mabel and the truth of it was, he was as well. He smiled a little at the thought of her round, cheerful face. She was the kind of old person who was always laughing and smiling. She knew some wicked jokes. Never sorry for herself, even though her husband had died ages ago – Danny only knew him from the photograph on the antique sideboard in the dining-room. The other thing about her was that she seemed to know everyone and everyone seemed to like her. And Jenny was right; she was a super cook. At the thought of Aunt Mabel's mouth-watering meals, so different from his mother's rather boring, almost always vegetarian ones, Danny began to cheer up. Who could he send a text to, now that Mark was off jaunting round the States? Ah Griff. He texted:

'Going on holiday to Lichfield. Top that!!!!' and pressed send.

A few seconds later, his phone began to vibrate but not with its usual tone: it was quite different from that. Danny shot upright, immediately alert. It was the signal that he had been waiting for – for at least six months. And now he almost couldn't believe that he was hearing the unmistakable pulse that meant that SHARP were contacting him. After months and months of silence, Kaz was getting in touch!

Danny pressed one of the buttons on his mobile that had not been there when he had bought it: one of three added by SHARP six months ago as the means for him to contact them or to be propelled backwards or forwards in time. As he knew it would, the screen slid away from the mobile, to hover a few feet in front of him, expanding to about the size of a 24 inch TV screen, the edges defined by a shiny black rim. A message was appearing in black letters on the background of swirling colours.

<Welcome once again Danny TO SHARP 15798>

You can put the mobile down now. The screen will stay in place until you press the black button again.

Danny placed the mobile on the floor beside him, never taking his eyes off the floating screen. The message faded. He watched as the background of intense swirling colours, that he remembered so well, seemed to spin off the screen into the air around him. Then the screen cleared for a moment and the following text appeared:

We must apologise to you for the interruption in our communications with you. All systems with your time zone were shut down for safety reasons. The safety of SHARP and therefore your safety was at risk.

That situation is now over and we are contacting you today in the hope that you will once again accept another travel option with us. Because there has been such a long time-lapse since we were last in touch, we will repeat some of our information and instructions. We do apologise if these are familiar to you.

Your safety is of the utmost importance to us and in almost all respects we can guarantee that you can travel backwards in time and return to your home time zone, without any ill effects whatsoever or any danger to yourself or the people you meet on your travels. However, every activity in life can result in danger, as I am sure you are aware, and so we cannot guarantee ultimate safety.

Danny read the words in front of him, even though he knew them almost by heart: they were the exact same words that he had read almost nine months ago when he had first been contacted and asked by SHARP to travel back to the time of the Stuarts and Tudors in England.

After you have read all the following, think about what we are asking you to do. All the instructions and communications after this come to you from Kazaresh, the student of our university who organised and guided your two previous trips. As before, Professor Aurelia Dobbs may also contact you from time to time.

Finally, we want you to know that your involvement with project 15798, for that is still the project that you are on, is very helpful to us, the remaining humankind of the world, and that, although it will be impossible for you to understand why, you will be making a contribution to the continuance of civilisation upon earth.

Our Company Policy is: Be of good hope and travel back in time and return in the spirit of greater good for all mankind.

The screen changed once more. This time, there was a countdown, with numbers flashing past the screen so quickly it was impossible to read them. At 2020 the numbers began to slow until they finally halted at 2010 and the following words appeared on the screen:

<INSTRUCTIONS to Danny Higgins from Kazaresh Porterman>

Kaz, the boy from the future who was not much older than he was but was already a university student at SHARP, and who had picked him to go on these missions back into the past, was getting in touch again! It was all Danny could do to stop a whoop of excitement escaping his mouth.

Hello Danny. It's great to be talking to you again. There have been a lot of difficulties this end and I wasn't involved at all – it was all the senior boffins and the very, very high techy people who run all our systems. I'm not really supposed to be telling you much, but the thing is, I couldn't even if I was allowed to, as I've no idea how half of that stuff works. The important thing is it's all sorted out now and everything is back to normal. We're back in business. Your previous missions to that mansion house Bramall Hall in 1615 and to Little Moreton Hall in 1554 were so successful, that of course SHARP want to use you again.

I've been told to send you the standard SHARP instructions again. I know you had them all last time but here they are, just in case you've forgotten, and remember, you can ask a short [very short] question by sending a text to SHARP 15798.

Hmmm thought Danny, I've tried texting you over and over the last few months but got no reply. I suppose it was because the systems were shut down until everything was secure again.

I will try to answer, truthfully, any questions you have although only one text is permitted in 24 hours and I won't be able to compromise SHARP protocols, and believe you me there are hundreds of new ones. It's like Health and Safety have taken over the whole outfit. I've only a few more assignments to reach full graduation and I'm a junior in the research department now. A lot of that was down to you and your success on your two trips. Here are all the instructions –

you've had them before but no harm in a little refresher course.

<Pre-Travel information>
When there is the possibility of a journey to a different time zone, the screen of your mobile will glow blue and you will feel a low-level vibration, different in pulse to its usual one. This may last for up to two hours, your time. After that the opportunity will have passed BUT do not be impatient. If it is not possible to take up the opportunity, there will be another one; they come along about every two or three days. You must fit travel around your normal life.

<Travel Information>
If you are ready to travel, make sure you are alone and somewhere where you will not be interrupted. You will be gone for between four to six minutes, your time. It will seem to you, when you are on a time journey, that you are away for much longer. It is not desirable for anyone to see you go or return. So make sure that no one is likely to be worried by your disappearance or will be looking for you. We must emphasize that

it is important that no one in your time zone knows anything about your involvement with SHARP.

Wearing clothes is not helpful so you will need to strip down to just underpants. You will have received from us a small bag that you must wear flush to your skin. It doesn't need ties or anything. When you have taken your clothes off, press the bag to your waist just above your underpants and it will stay there. Do this BEFORE you press the green button to go. The bag contains a small silver disc which you must put on your forehead when you arrive. The disc is almost weightless so you will not notice it but it will record everything you see. It only activates when it is worn, and it only lasts a short while, so do not put it on until AFTER you arrive in the past. On your arrival, take the disc out and press it to your forehead. The backing disc will come away. Put this and your phone into the bag and secure the fastening. You'll find that the bag attaches itself to your skin without any discomfort. It cannot be taken from you and assures your safe return. (I know, I know you've worn one before – but rules are rules and right now they say I've got to tell you this stuff all over again].

<Journey>

When you are ready to go, key in the project number 15798 and press the black button. A screen will appear that will tell you where you are going, what you will see and who you will meet. It identifies a Destination. This is not necessarily where you land but the place that SHARP has planned for you to visit. Read these travel instructions very carefully and when you are sure you have understood them, key in the project number 15798 and then press the green button. The system will be activated and you will be transported back in time.

When you arrive in the past, there will be a pile of clothes nearby that are suitable for the time and place, and you must put these on as quickly as possible.

The people you meet will either mistake you for someone they know or will not be surprised that a stranger is with them. On your journeys you will find that you can help people; this you should do. Never do anything unkind.

<Return Journey>

When it is time for you to return, you will feel the phone vibrating. You will have to take off the clothes that you've been wearing and leave them in a pile, preferably somewhere they cannot be seen too easily. Take the phone out of the bag and press the red button. If you need to return because of danger before the phone vibrates, key in 15798, remove the clothes as described above and press the red button. This should only be done under extreme emergency conditions.

<After Your Visit>

We will contact you after your visit, to give you an assessment of how well you have done in providing information and living in the time zone which you have visited. We are able to access any part of your computer, so if you would like to write a record about your journey, that would be very helpful but we know you have school work, so if you do not want to do that, that is fine. We know that you have written about your previous time journey on MySpace and suggest that you do the same on any other social networking site, such as Facebook. People will assume it is only a story you have made up but if any other kids travel back in time, they might read what you have written and contact you. Be sure you NEVER reveal that the people you meet from the future have seven fingers. That is of utmost importance.

We will be sending you a blue screen with an option for travel in the next few days. If you do not take up the option for this or the next two option times, we will assume that you have decided not to take part in our project and we will return your mobile to its original state and retrieve our travel bag. As you have now completed two successful trips you are entitled to use the letters 'Xr' after your name. These are the first two letters of the word xrosmonaut (It's a shortened form of the word chrosmonaut from the word chronology.) It is the term we use for someone who time-travels successfully. To have the full word after your name is a great honour.

'Wow I've got letters after my name. Like I've done a degree or something.' Danny spoke out loud. He was so chuffed about his new status. His dad and mum both had letters after their names but didn't use them, although his dad, having slogged away for several years to get an MA used them occasionally when he wanted to impress someone. The screen cleared and then after a few moments the words appeared:

Goodbye for now Danny, remember you can text me, Kaz.

The floating screen immediately shrank back to fit its normal space on the mobile.

Danny felt excitement bubbling inside him – no need to feel in the least bit jealous of Mark now. Going to America for two weeks was pretty ordinary stuff compared to being the only person on the planet to travel through time! It was an awesome thought. Just at the moment the awesome–ness of it was all located in his stomach. There was a very strange feeling in his stomach that could only be described by the totally stupid expression that his mum used: 'butterflies in the tummy'. It was like he had dozens of them all fluttering and buttering in there. Danny keyed in 15798 and,

even though his hands were shaking a bit, he quickly
sent the text:

> congrats on your progress to the research de-
> partment. Im mostest chuffed @ the letters
> after my name. Wot's this about another kid T
> travelling? And any idea where or when I might
> be going? Oh and I'll never tell anyone that you
> are a seven-fingered weirdo! Danny

The message was sent and a reply text came in
from Kaz:

> Thanks for the congrats. SHARP are thinking
> about another kid, some girl, I think . But for you
> – not sure yet of where or when, but does Lich-
> field mean anything? For us, five fingers is seri-
> ously weird! Kaz.

Whoaho ...LICHFIELD, Danny was amazed. As
with all communications from Kaz or SHARP, the message was not saved on his phone and faded quickly.
Just then a text from Griff came in, telling him he was
going on holiday to Centre Parks in the Lake District
so he reckoned that that topped Danny's holiday des-

tination. Obviously he hadn't understood that Danny had been using irony in his message. 'Griff's a thicko,' thought Danny 'but who cares?' He bounded down the stairs and into the kitchen.

'Hey guys, what day are we off to Aunt Mabel's?'

'You've changed your tune,' said his mum.

CHAPTER 2

Half A Message

They didn't set off for Lichfield until Tuesday. Mr Higgins wasn't sure he was going to be able to get the time off. But in the end it all worked out well. He was working on an area of historical research that related to the whole of the midland area with a team of other academics and it turned out that some of the records that needed to be looked at were to be found on the sacrists' roll at Lichfield Cathedral. His colleagues were all happy for Mr. Higgins to take on this research. So he came in from work on Friday all smiles.

'They've allowed me four days off next week; well not 'off' exactly but in Lichfield. I'll need to go in Monday, just to sort out exactly what we want to look at and let Dr Richardson in Lichfield know that I am coming. But we'll be able to set off early Tuesday a.m.'

'Does that mean that you'll be working dad – you won't be able go places with us?' asked Jenny.

'Ye…s, I will be working most of the day but I'll catch up with you all in the evening.'

'You won't be too sorry about that, will you Dad?'

put in Danny.

'What makes you say that Danny?' asked his mum.

'Well you know how Dad and Aunt Mabel are always arguing.' Danny grinned, enjoying winding his parents up.

'Danny!' His mum was shocked.

'Aunt Mabel and I don't argue. We just…we just…' Mr Higgins was fumbling for the right thing to say and looking a bit embarrassed.

'It's true – it's true!' Jenny, sensing the fun, joined in. 'You and Aunt Mabel had that hu…uge argument about whose car was the greenest.'

'That's right,' Danny said. 'You were saying ours was the most eco-friendly and Aunt Mabel said that her old Rover was much greener because it was diesel and diesel was a more efficient fuel than petrol.'

'Well Aunt Mabel doesn't know what she's talking about,' snapped Dad, and then hastily covered up this criticism of an adult with: 'well, when she's talking about cars that is. Trouble is she's just fond of that old Rover of hers. Anyway that wasn't an argument. We were just exchanging ideas.'

'Oh and then there was the Aga argument,' Danny wasn't going to let his dad off the hook…

'The Aga argument!' exclaimed Mum. 'They have an Aga argument every time we've stayed with Aunt Mabel. I think the first one must have been before we were married. Your Dad and I went to stay with Aunt Mabel when we were at university together and had just got engaged.'

'Did Aunt Mabel approve of you choosing Dad?' asked Jenny, always intrigued by the time in her parents' life before she and Danny were born.

'I don't think she did,' Mum and Dad said in unison, which kind of proved the point. Even though they were both laughing, Jenny's question introduced a serious note into the conversation because Mrs Higgins's parents had died when she was quite young, just a teenager, so it would have been important what Aunt Mabel, her mother's sister, thought of a prospective husband.

'Anyway I don't argue about the Aga on green issues,' said Mr. Higgins hastily moving the conversation on. 'You know, don't you Rachel? – I'm just being practical about it. An old lady of seventy-odd can't keep on filling a stove with solid fuel. What happens if she gets ill? Who will keep the Aga alight?'

'I know, I know Simon – you're right.' Danny and Jenny gravitated towards the TV as the conversation got boringly fixed on the needs and difficulties of the elderly. Neither Jenny nor Danny wanted to think of Aunt Mabel as old. They knew she was, but that's different to wanting to know all the ins and outs.

By one o'clock Tuesday, the Higgins family were ready for the off, packed into their medium-sized, relatively new, family estate car. Dad had fished out his petrol notebook and recorded the mileage before they set off. This was part of his car-driving routine. He recorded the petrol consumption of his car meticulously so that should it go up in any way he could have the garage investigate as soon as possible.

Danny and Jenny settled down in the back, Danny with his DS and Jenny with nothing to do but stare out of the window, because doing anything else made her feel more car-sick than she usually did, even if she had had a travel sickness pill. They lived in Bisley, a small town fifteen miles north of Nottingham where Mr. H worked at the university. It took only ten minutes or so to get on to the main road and soon Mr. H was driving at a steady 45 miles an hour. This was, he was fond of saying, the optimum speed for petrol consumption and he could never understand why other drivers went any faster. As he said the words:

'If everyone drove at this speed, think of the difference it would make to global warming.' Danny mouthed the words in the back to Jenny who gave him a smile that managed to convey: 'I know – Dad's a bore, but he's right.'

The only two eventful things that happened on the way was a lay-by stop for Jenny to get out and be sick, with mum standing by with handfuls of wipes, and Danny's mobile starting to vibrate with the pulse that told him that the people at SHARP were contacting him. When Jenny got back in, they drove off with all the windows open because of the strong whiff of sick. The phone was still vibrating when they drove into the quiet street that led down to Aunt Mabel's big old rambling house.

As they were all getting out of the car, the front door opened and out flew Rocket followed by the stout figure of Aunt Mabel.

Much smiling, laughing and telling Aunt Mabel about Jenny being sick followed. Rocket jumped up and licked everyone and Aunt Mabel wrapped everyone in a big, firm hug.

Inside, the grandfather clock still counted the seconds with its loud tick, the dark brown antique furniture still shone from its beeswax polish and Aunt

Mabel's interesting clutter still piled up wherever: on the seats of chairs, in corners and on the small tables. In the sitting room a delicious tea was laid out. There was lemon drizzle cake, iced buns and Victoria jam sponge. Despite such gorgeous nosh, Danny couldn't stop thinking about his phone still vibrating in his pocket. It would be so interesting just to see where SHARP intended sending him. He was wondering if he could politely escape and have a quick peak at his phone when the perfect idea popped into his head.

'Dad, I'll go and get the cases in if you like.'

'Good lad,' said dad who had just poured himself another cup of tea.

'Put your mum's and dad's case in the first bedroom on the right, Jenny's in the little room at the bottom of the hall and you're in the room on the top floor,' explained Aunt Mabel.

'Got that. No worries. I'll get it sorted.'

'Such a grown up lad now,' smiled Aunt Mabel as Danny left the room.

He dashed out to the car. He needed two trips; one with his parents' case and one with Jenny's small bag and his own. He dumped the bags on the floor as quickly as he could and then went to the bathroom, locking the door behind him. He pressed the black information button on his phone. The screen slid away and enlarged as usual, filled with a bright intense blue and then with swirling colours that slowly dimmed. The message appeared.

Hello Danny here are the instructions for your next journey.

<Time zone>
January..........

That was it. He waited. Several minutes went past and nothing moved on the screen.

'Danny, are you in there? Are you coming to walk Rocket with me?' Jenny was knocking on the door.

'Sure, give me a minute, I'll be down.'

Danny pressed the black button and the screen slid back to its normal size. That was odd, very odd, thought Danny.

CHAPTER 3

A Proper Breakfast

One of the best things about staying at Aunt Mabel's was breakfast. On the first morning of their visit, Danny joined the rest of the family sitting round the huge table in the middle of the kitchen and grinned at everyone in anticipation. He could easily have been transported back in time, he thought, no intervention of any scientists from the future needed – there was not much about the twenty-first century in Aunt Mabel's kitchen.

Copper pans hung on the walls or were stacked high on shelves; bunches of dried herbs hung on hooks; a large dresser at one side of the room displayed Aunt Mabel's precious collection of Staffordshire china: delicately hand-painted plates, cups, and jugs. There was something called the 'pantry' (whatever that was) door behind which were rows and rows of Aunt Mabel's neatly labelled home-made jam. Pride of place was taken by the magnificent Aga, a huge cast-iron solid fuel stove. It kept the kitchen warm all the time; cosy in winter but sometimes a bit too hot in summer. On a summer's day, first thing in the morning Aunt Mabel would open the back door so you could sit in the kitchen and see right down the garden path to the fields at the back where cattle were grazing. That morning it was open and bright sunlight was streaming in. Rocket dozed outside on the doormat, one ear cocked at the goings-on inside.

At the Aga, Aunt Mabel was cooking breakfast for the family – one frying pan crispy bacon and

sausages, while in the other eggs spluttered one by one as Aunt Mabel cracked them in, flipped them over and, with a deft turn of the wrist, landed them on the next plate. Like an inspired conductor directing the orchestra, she controlled the whole production of breakfast; wouldn't hear of anyone helping, and only sat down to eat her own when everyone else was served. Nobody, but nobody muttered a word about a full English breakfast not being healthy.

When Dad had put his knife and fork down and wiped his plate round with the last bit of crusty bread (an action that amused both Jenny and Danny who had often heard him denounce the eating of such fatty foods at breakfast as 'a death warrant'), he said:

'That was delicious, Mabel. But I suppose I'd better get moving; I've got a meeting with Dr Richardson in the archive office at 10 o'clock. What are you lot up to today? Are you going to visit the cathedral?'

'Not today,' said Aunt Mabel.

'Well, when you do go, I'd like Danny to have a good look round to see if he can spot any 'green men'. There are quite a few, I think, in Lichfield Cathedral aren't there Mabel?'

'Mmm, yes. I think you may be right there, Simon.'

'Green men? What on earth are they?' asked Jenny.

'You remember. Dad showed us one on the outside of that house called Bramall Hall. It was carved in wood.'

'Goodness Danny, I'm surprised you remembered that,' butted in his dad. 'It's almost a year ago now we called at that place and we didn't even go inside. I'd forgotten the name of it, completely – though I do remember the carving.'

Of course Danny remembered it: it was the place he visited the first time he time-travelled! He'd gone back to the year 1615 and stood outside that mansion house looking up at that carving of a strange head with leaves coming out of its mouth with a boy who must have been born at least 300 years before. It was not something he was going to forget!

Fortunately no one noticed that Danny didn't respond to his dad's surprise because they were all too busy explaining to Jenny that 'green men' were believed to be pagan symbols that Christians in early times, incorporated into their own religion and sometimes included in their designs of churches and cathedrals. Then Aunt Mabel asked more about the mansion house Danny had mentioned.

'It's a lovely old black and white Cheshire Eliza-
bethan mansion. You'd love it. We've been meaning to
go back. It's just on the outskirts of Manchester, a
rather nice suburb called Bramhall.' Mrs Higgins went
on for some time about the house and its family.
Danny started to be amused at the thought that he
could correct her on some historical facts. For instance,
he knew that her insistence on calling the building
'black and white' wasn't really accurate as it had been
a decidedly muddy brown colour when he had seen
it, not so long after it had been built.

Feeling a paw scratching at her leg, Jenny said:

'Rocket wants us to go for a walk.'

'Oh do take him, there's good children,' Aunt
Mabel held out his lead. Jenny and Danny escaped
with the dog to the footpath at the back of the house
that led through into fields. Danny was glad to get
away from the grown-ups for a while; he needed time
to think. Why had he been contacted by SHARP yesterday with such a scrambled message? Why hadn't
SHARP sent the travel bag if they wanted him to go
on a trip back in time? Had the problems that Kaz had
told him about really been sorted out? And most im-
portantly what would he decide to do if they did send
him a proper travel option? Would it be wise to go – to

risk it? Even as he formed the question in his head, he knew what his answer would be. No matter what, he would go. What was it about risks?

Jenny, who had been throwing an old rubber ring for a scampering Rocket to fetch, suddenly rushed up to him and said:

'Do you know where we're going today?'

'No idea – Do you?'

'I heard Aunt Mabel and mum discussing it before everyone came down for breakfast. But they don't know I heard, so don't tell them.'

'Well where then?'

'Somewhere scary. Guess.'

'Scary? You mean like in scary rides?'

'Yes.'

'Was it Drayton Manor Theme Park?'

'Yes it was. Have you heard of it?'

'Mmm, one of the guys at school, not Mark, went a couple of months ago. He said the rides were wicked. There's one called...now what did he say the name was? Oh, I think it was Apocalypse – it sounded good, I mean really good. Come on, let's get back.'

'Don't let Mum and Aunt Mabel know that I've told you.'

'Oh Jenny, you worry far too much about hurting other people's feelings – it's not right for someone of your age.'

'Plea…ease, Danny.'

'Course I won't.'

When they got back to the house, Dad had left for Lichfield and Mum and Aunt Mabel were ready to set out. Aunt Mabel was looking very pleased with herself. She explained that she had been given tickets to Drayton Manor Theme Park by a friendly neighbour.

'Wicked,' said Danny.

'Fabulous!' exclaimed Jenny, both managing a very good effort at surprised delight.

'Why do people always give you things?' asked Jenny.

'I've no idea.'

'It's because she always does so much for others,' said their mum.

They piled into Aunt Mabel's old Rover 75 Tourer, and as soon as they were out of the side roads, Aunt Mabel put her foot down on the accelerator so that nearly all the way to Tamworth she exceeded Dad's optimum 45 miles an hour, and strangely Jenny did not feel in the least bit sick.

When they arrived at the theme park, there was

a slight hitch as Aunt Mabel's large handbag, into which she stuffed every conceivable item she might need on a journey, seemed to have eaten up the family ticket. She emptied everything out twice into Mum's open hands and, just as Danny was beginning to lose hope of ever getting through the gates, the tickets were located and all the other items rammed back into the bag.

'Are you going on any rides?' Jenny asked her mum and Aunt Mabel. They both shook their heads.

Jenny didn't meet the height restrictions for the most extreme rides so Danny went with her on the rides like Splash Canyon and Buffalo Coaster. Even these less extreme rides got them both shrieking and laughing hysterically. There was a lot of queuing but no one minded and the warm June weather made the hours zip by.

'I'd really like to go on the Apocalypse, Mum. Jenny can't come; she's too small.'

'I'd hate to, anyway, Danny. I don't know how you could think of going on that; it looks awful.'

'Jenny can wait with us, while you go on it, Danny. Are you sure you really want to?'

'Mmm. Yes, I do. The Apocalypse looks awesome.'

'OK. We'll wait for you here. We'll get Jenny an ice cream.'

As he queued, Danny thought, 'I bet all these people would sign up for going on the SHARP experience, if they knew about it. No matter how safe we try to make life, some people seem to crave danger. It must be hard-wired into our personalities.'

Just as Danny was getting into his place on the ride, his phone started vibrating. 'Well, SHARP – there's no way I can take this call,' he thought. The ride filled up and, without any warning, started. Within a few seconds, Danny felt as if he had left his stomach way, way behind and the most terrifying force seemed to catapult him into the sky. How long the ride lasted, he couldn't say, all he knew was that he was very glad when it was over and his shaking legs took him back to where Jenny, Mum and Aunt Mabel all hugged him as if he had returned from the battle front.

'Everyone ready for something to eat?' asked Aunt Mabel, leading the way to the car park. Danny realised that his phone had stopped vibrating. 'I wonder if the people at SHARP were hit by shock waves as I hurtled through space on the Apocalypse? But then how fast must I travel through time to go back hundreds of years? Maybe when you go through time it's different to going through space – you'd have to study physics, to know the answer to that.'

They went to a pizza place that Aunt Mabel knew, and oh what a surprise – the restaurant-owner knew Aunt Mabel. Did she know everyone in a twenty-mile radius of Lichfield? The pizzas tasted more delicious than any Danny could remember.

'Funny how fear makes you so hungry,' he said.

'Well, I must have had vicarious fear then,' said Mum, 'cos I'm starving.'

'Errr… what's vicarious mean, mum?'

'Experiencing something for someone else. I was probably in much more of a state than you were when you went on that last shocker.'

'Right, vicarious; I'll remember that.'

'What's dad going to have for tea?' Jenny asked.

'Oh we'll take him one of these home,' said Aunt Mabel.

'But Dad never eats takeaway.'

'Well, he will tonight,' said Mum and Aunt Mabel together, a look of triumph on their faces.

'He'll be able to vicariously enjoy our afternoon,' chipped in Danny.

'Careful Danny Higgins, or you'll turn into a nerd,' said Aunt Mabel.

'Oh, he's one of those, on the quiet,' said Mum. 'You would never believe how interested in history he's become.'

Danny pulled a face. Didn't grown-ups realise how irritating they could be?

CHAPTER 4

The Cathedral

The next day's planned activity couldn't have been more different from those of the day at the theme park. They were going into Lichfield. After breakfast just before Jenny and Danny took Rocket on his morning walk, Mum explained that Aunt Mabel wanted her to go to the estate agent's with her.

'Why? Why the estate agent?' Danny and Jenny both asked the same question.

'Because, she's going to sell this house and get somewhere smaller.'

'No,' said Jenny. 'She can't, she can't sell this house.'

Mrs Higgins did her best to explain.

'Aunt Mabel is getting much too old to look after a rambling old place like this, Jenny. She needs something modern, easy to run.' Jenny didn't want to listen. She ran out of the back door with Rocket at her heels. Danny caught up with her half way down the footpath.

'I've never seen you look so sulky, Jen.'

'I'm not sulky.'

'You look sulky.'

'Well it's OK for you. You don't care. You didn't even want to come this time.' Jenny looked near to tears. Danny didn't say anything for several minutes. He just walked along beside her. He was trying to do his older brother understanding bit.

'You know, everything changes in life – nothing stays the same.' This lofty philosophical thought, despite Danny being proud of it, didn't seem to have much of an effect on Jenny.

'I love Aunt Mabel's house.'

'I know you do, but Jenny don't you love Aunt Mabel more than her house? If she keeps on living here, she might not last too long. You know, if you let Aunt Mabel know how upset you are at the idea of her selling, she might not do it and then how would feel if she got ill through trying to look after the house?' Danny was going heavy on the psychology. Jenny seemed to calm down a bit; she even picked up a few sticks to throw for Rocket, having forgotten to bring his ring.

'If they're going to estate agents and things like that, what are we going to do?' she asked.

'I rather think the idea is for us to go to the Cathedral – you because you want to do some sketching, and me to search for any references to green men in the architecture like dad said. You said you wanted to do another picture for Aunt Mabel because of that really pathetic one you did when you were really little.'

'Oh that awful thing that looks like three squashed-in pyramids – she's still got it in the hall – it's terrible.'

'Well do her a better one.'

When they got back to the house, Mum looked at Jenny enquiringly and Jenny gave her a weak, watery smile to show that she was trying to get used to the idea of Aunt Mabel moving.

Everyone got ready for the off. Jenny put her sketching things into her school back pack; Aunt Mabel and Mum, who had been making a picnic while the children walked the dog, carried a picnic hamper out to the car and Danny put a small notebook and pencil into the pocket of his shorts. He patted his other pocket to make sure his mobile was there. Aunt Mabel backed her old but still magnificent Rover Tourer 75

They were soon entering Lichfield Cathedral Close.

'It just says 'The Close' on the name plate,' said Jenny.

'Well everyone in Lichfield knows that if you say 'The Close' you mean 'the Cathedral Close,' said Aunt Mabel. She jammed on the brakes so suddenly that if they hadn't been wearing seat belts there might have been some banged heads. She wound down the window (no such thing as electrically operated ones in the days when the Rover was made) and stuck her head out.

'Uhoo, Henry, ' she hailed a black-suited figure who stopped and turned to look and see who had called to him. He spotted the Rover and crossed over

the road.

'Nice to see you, Mabel. How are you?'

'You see I told you Aunt Mabel knows everyone in a twenty mile radius of Lichfield,' whispered Danny.

'Fine, I'm absolutely fine. I wonder if you could do me a favour?' Aunt Mabel got out of the car and motioned to Danny and Jenny to do the same.

'This is my great nephew and niece. Jenny is very keen on sketching and is going into the Cathedral to see if there are some things she would like to draw, and Danny is interested in the history of the building. Danny and Jenny, this is our head verger.' They shook hands, and the head verger beamed at them.

'Their mother and I are just off into the town. We'll be back to pick them up in about an hour. Could you just keep an eye on them for us?'

'No bother at all. Mabel.'

The old Rover turned out of the close and Danny and Jenny followed the head verger towards the front door.

'The Open Door folk are just setting up their 'activities fortnight', so there'll be lots to see and all the helpers are friendly folk – you can ask them any questions you like and they will try to answer you.'

The head verger led the way up the steps of the

south transept and into the calm and solemn splendour of the great building. Its vaulting roof and mighty pillars took the eye upward, as if to heaven.

'Wow. It's much bigger than I remember,' whispered Jenny. She felt she had to whisper, even though there were a lot of people coming and going and none of them seemed to bother too much to keep their voices especially quiet.

'It probably looks much bigger because we have removed all the chairs,' said the verger.

'Is it alright for me to wander round and see what I want to sketch?' asked Jenny.

'Of course.'

'I'm going to do the same, wander round but I'm going to be looking for 'green men,' said Danny. 'My dad has asked me to find them and note whereabouts there are in the cathedral.'

'See that desk over there young man? I think you will find that they have some leaflets showing a floor plan of the cathedral – you could use it to mark on any you find. They might have some other information you would find useful as well'

'Oh thanks, a plan of the cathedral would be a great help.'

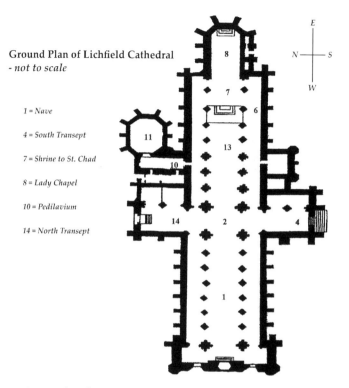

Ground Plan of Lichfield Cathedral
- not to scale

1 = *Nave*

4 = *South Transept*

7 = *Shrine to St. Chad*

8 = *Lady Chapel*

10 = *Pedilavium*

14 = *North Transept*

Jenny had spotted a piece of sculpture called 'The Sleeping Children,' 'That's lovely,' she thought 'but quite difficult to do,' and she moved further down.

The verger said he would need to leave them now, but if they needed anything to ask the 'Welcomer'a person wearing a blue gown who was always to be found at the West End.

Danny made his way to the desk that the verger had pointed out to him and got the floor plan. He chatted to the lady for a bit and she gave him a few tips on how to locate the green men and an information leaflet about how to explore the cathedral. He caught up with Jenny sitting in front of a sculpture that she proudly told him had been done by Jacob Epstein. It was a bronze head of someone called 'Bishop Woods'.

'Whatever floats your boat, Jenny' said Danny. He often puzzled about his sister who sometimes seemed so serious and so wrapped up in her art. Was she going to be a real geek by the time she was eleven? – Mmm possibly.

'Anyway who was Jacob Epstein? Or come to that Bishop Woods?'

'I don't really know,' said Jenny but a lady told me that Jacob Epstein was a very famous sculptor, even famous in America.

'You know, it's lucky there's those nice red cushions on those seats, else your bum would get as cold as the stone you're sitting on.'

'Danny!' exclaimed Jenny, indignant that he should use the word 'bum' in the cathedral.

'Well Miss Cleversticks, it says here that those stone seats are called 'pedalavium' which is Latin for feet washing. I leave you with this thought and go in search of Dad's green men.'

A bit further on Danny found a green man at the top of one of the huge columns. It was hidden in the mass of carved stone leaves that circled the column some twenty feet up. He certainly would not have spotted it if the lady at the desk had not told him where to look. She had said that it was the face of William de Ramsay, the King's Master Mason depicted by one of his disgruntled workers out of spite.

Danny smiled at the thought that it was best not to get on the wrong side of a talented stone-carver who could commemorate your grumpiness for all to see for the next millennium.

As the leaflet suggested, he continued clockwise and came to a small chapel.

He decided that it must be the Lady Chapel – there were a great many statues of ladies, so that sort of clinched it. For some reason, two women were putting some brown garments out on the backs of chairs. Danny stood watching, wondering what they were doing.

'We'll need to break for lunch soon,' one of them said.

'Well yes, but let's make sure everything is ready for this afternoon,' the other replied, and then looked over and noticed Danny. 'Hello young man, are you wondering what's going on here?'

'Well, yes, I was actually.' Danny approached a bit nearer.

The woman held out one of the garments.

'These are the kind of clothes pilgrims would have worn when coming to the shrine of St. Chad. Would you care to try it on?'

Danny gave a grin: 'It doesn't look my style, but if you insist.' He didn't want to offend the ladies, so he hunched into the cloak and the woman showed him how to pull the hood up over his head.

'Oh, now he's a real Holy Hoodie,' the first one said, and they both laughed. Danny played along and bowed his head, the cloak almost obscuring his face. Then, a bit embarrassed, he threw the hood back, slipped the cloak off and handed it back.

'Who were the pilgrims?'

'They were just ordinary people who walked many, many miles to worship at special holy places, and the site of Lichfield Cathedral was a very special holy place. These are pale imitations of a real pilgrim's cloak, of course. They would have been made from very thick, warm woollen material to keep the pilgrim alive through cold frosty nights. Many pilgrims who made their way to Lichfield would have had to sleep out at night. Perhaps they couldn't afford to stay in an inn, or possibly when night fell, they would be far distant from any habitation. They would find what shelter they could, wrap their cloak round them and fall asleep under the stars.'

The picture she painted was so vivid, Danny almost shivered at the thought of being one of those pilgrims sleeping rough. 'Well thanks,' he said. 'I've learnt something I didn't know before.'

'That's what we're here for, young man,' one said over her shoulder as they both hurried off down the South Choir Aisle to get their lunch.

When they had gone, the whole cathedral seemed strangely quiet, and then Danny heard something: something familiar – a high-pitched whine getting nearer and nearer, louder and louder until it completely filled his ears. He put his hands up and tried to block out the sound. Then he stumbled forward as if thumped on the back. He grabbed a chair to steady himself but there seemed to be nothing there: he was left clutching a pilgrim's cloak. The vast roof of the cathedral was bearing down on him, getting closer as if to crush him, and then …Nothing.

CHAPTER 5

Praying For His Life

When Danny came to, he was lying face downwards, but not on the floor of the Lady Chapel. He was lying on the ground, his arms outstretched, and he was very, very cold. He curled the fingers of one of his hands and scrunched dry, crisp leaves: leaves that had fallen from a tree months ago and were now covered in a thick rime of frost. In the other hand he could feel that he was still holding the pilgrim's cloak.

'I've time travelled.' Danny said the words out loud to the black earth beneath his face. With great difficulty he rolled over and looked up at the sky. There were dark, grey, lowering clouds above him and he estimated that it must be late afternoon; late afternoon in the winter when the light was going to fade quickly. He struggled into a sitting position, shivering violently from the cold that was spiking in through his thin summer T–shirt and lightweight trousers, as if he had nothing on.

Then he became aware of a strange thundering coming up from the ground beneath him. He turned to his left, and saw a herd of deer with hooves flying, racing straight towards him. He scrambled to his feet, still clutching the cloak from the cathedral, and staggered back to the shelter of a clump of stunted trees and bushes. He got behind a tree just in time to save himself from the thundering hooves of the frightened animals. He shuddered when he saw what had sent the deer into a panic: close on their heels pounded wolves, their jaws agape, their tongues hanging out, snapping and snarling at the nearest deer. As he watched in fascinated horror, the animals disappeared some way off, down a dip in the ground. Danny couldn't see them for a while, but they re-emerged, now a good distance away. The wolves had separated one of the deer from the herd and soon they brought it down. The eerie sound of their barking, calling to tell others of their kill, faintly reached his ears. Where was he and in what time period?

The fear of being trampled to death seemed to have brought him to his senses a little; he realised he was holding the pilgrim's cloak from the cathedral. 'Must put it on, must put the pilgrim's cloak on – it will give me some protection from the biting cold.' But before he could put the cloak on, his throat clenched. With a horrible, queasy feeling his stomach revolted and the next minute he was yukking up. 'Oh my goodness! Oh my goodness… I'm in a bad way!'

'Something has gone very wrong. It must be something to do with SHARP; they've messed up big time. I'm not going to survive… I'm going to die! SHARP have sent me back in time but with no preparation, no travel programme, no travel bag.'

He felt in his pocket and his shaking hand closed over his mobile. For a moment, he felt a surge of hope. He looked at the screen. It was black. He pressed the red emergency button. The screen remained black. Nothing – no activation – nothing. He kept on pressing the button again and again, as if that was going to make a difference. Only a fragment of common sense stopped him from smashing the mobile onto the ground. Sheer panic, made worse by the horrible taste of sick in his mouth, paralysed him; he had no idea what to do next. Then the thought of the wolves coming back to find another dinner spurred him into action. To calm himself down, he started talking to himself.

'Don't be such a wuss. Jenny was sick by the roadside the other day. You know how much she hates that, but you didn't think twice about it because she recovered and that's what you'll do. Stop being a wuss.

Put the cloak on.'

Luckily, the cloak hadn't trailed in the sick. He stepped away from the patch of grass where his morning breakfast was splattered, and struggled to get the cloak round him. It wasn't thick. He remembered the lady in the cathedral telling him that the real pilgrims' cloaks would have been much thicker. Even so, with it tightly wrapped round him and the hood over his head, he began to feel a bit warmer.

He looked around. Behind were the trees that had saved him. A thin layering of snow outlined the bare winter branches, and frost, untouched by the warmth of any daytime sun, whitened the ground. A landscape of rough pasture stretched away on all sides as far as he could see, with no houses breaking the monotony. But, through the sparse trees he could make out a low, dry-stone wall – a sign of human habitation! He walked towards it. The wall was curved and only short. It went nowhere but seemed to mark out a large clearing; the grass was flattened by many feet and there were two distinct paths leading away to left and right.

He was just trying to think where he should head to next, when he heard something: the sound of voices, not talking, not shouting but deep voices in unison –

chanting. The sound was far off to start with but it got louder; the voices were getting nearer. He didn't know whether to stay or run away to hide – but where? The chanting seemed to be coming from all sides. Then from left and right, groups of people appeared; they began gathering in the clearing. They took no notice of Danny at all. All of them were dressed in long cloaks and they all had their hoods pulled up over their heads. Danny realised that the reason they took no notice of him, was that he must have looked like one of them. He could see though, even in the fading light, that their cloaks were much thicker than his and they were mud-splattered and dirty. As the people gathered, the chanting began to slow. Danny could identify one word, one sound over and above the others. He did not understand it at all: they seemed to be repeating over and over:

'Chedda, chedda!'

Then suddenly there was silence. Towards the assembled people walked a man carrying in front of him a stick, curled over at the top like a shepherd's crook. On either side walked two others. The three wore the long pilgrims' cloaks, but their hoods were thrown back and they each had a wooden crucifix hanging around their necks. As they stopped in front of the gathering, everyone fell to their knees, Danny as well. It was obvious that these were holy people. Were they monks? The leader, although short in terms of modern men, was the tallest. He started talking to the people kneeling in front of him. His voice was crystal clear and rang out in the cold evening air.

At first, Danny couldn't understand a word the monk was saying but gradually he began to pick out one or two words that he thought he recognised: was that the word 'good?' and had he heard the word 'evil?' Because of the strangeness of the speech, Danny began to calculate that he must have gone back in time to a very early period. Was this Old English he was hearing? Despite himself, Danny couldn't help being interested in the people around him. He peered sideways at the man to his left who kept coughing, a short, rasping cough that made it hard for him to join in the responses, even though he tried. Then to his right, Danny noticed black curls escaping the hood of a small dumpy figure – could that be a girl? But most of all his eyes were drawn to those of the monk who was speaking. His face was old but in some way that Danny couldn't explain, a shining goodness seemed to come from his eyes.

The man's voice changed. It became softer. He

put his hands together and bowed his head. 'He's saying a prayer,' Danny thought. Then the words:

> *'Feder ure du cart in heofenum*
> *se din noma is gehalgad…'*

Although, many of the words were unknown to
him, Danny was sure that what he was hearing was an
Old English version of the Lord's Prayer.

The monk blessed the kneeling people with the
sign of the cross. He opened his arms as if embracing
them all, and the people got to their feet. As they did
so, they blocked Danny's view of the monk with the
shepherd's crook. He could just tell that he, and the
two who had come with him, were turning to go. He
felt an overpowering urge to see the monk's face again,
to see him close to. He moved forward, pushing himself through the crowd who were now talking, chat-
ting amongst themselves, like a church congregation
after the service is over. While he had knelt together
with the other people, the desperation that had en-
gulfed him earlier, had seeped away, but now it began
to grip him again – he must look at the monk's face one
more time.

The monk who had started down a path when
Danny emerged from the crowd, stopped, said something to his two companions and turned to walk back

towards him. The light from his eyes seemed to send warmth into Danny's now nearly frozen limbs. As Danny looked into the kind, gentle eyes he felt a surge of hope. The monk began to say something. Danny heard the words, and tried to make out their meaning but then another sound came: it was the whine that came whenever he was going to travel through time. It was zinging in his ears, blotting out the sound of the monk's voice. Danny could feel his mind spinning in the sound and then ...Nothing.

CHAPTER 6

Hypothermia

When Danny next opened his eyes, he could see the blurred shapes of faces leaning over him. He heard a moaning sound, and then realised that he was the one moaning. He tried to stop it but couldn't. He pressed the flat of his hands on the ground and thought: 'stone, not rough grass, stone slabs – I'm back – I'm back on the floor of the Lady Chapel in Lichfield Cathedral'. Somehow SHARP had got him back.

Gradually the faces above him began to take shape; the two ladies whom he had met in the chapel were looking anxiously down at him.

'It was a good job we came back for an umbrella or we wouldn't have found him…. Found him…found him.' The words echoed around Danny's brain and his eyes closed, drifting him back into unconsciousness. Then he opened them again and now it was Jenny's voice he could hear:

'His hands are freezing cold – they're like blocks of ice!' He could tell there was panic in her voice, but he couldn't see her – was she kneeling beside him?

There was another voice, a man's voice: was it the head verger?

'We must get some blankets and the stretcher trolley.'

'Well,' Danny thought – 'the cathedral seems all geared up to rescuing people returned from... from when?'

What century had he been in? Whenever it was, it had been dreadfully cold and he was still cold through and through, as if nothing would ever warm him up again. He was vaguely aware of being lifted on to the trolley and blankets being tucked round him; they didn't seem to do anything to unfreeze him and unconsciousness claimed him again.

While Danny lay on the stretcher like a dead body, Jenny was struggling very hard not to cry. People kept asking her questions that she couldn't answer. She couldn't remember mum's mobile number, or when Mum and Aunt Mabel said they would get back to the cathedral. She just kept saying: 'I don't know.' Then she suddenly realized that these cathedral people would know Dr Richardson. Jumbled words tumbling from her mouth, she managed to explain that her dad was visiting Dr Richardson. The cathedral librarian knew Dr Richardson well, so rang and explained that

Danny, the son of his visitor, Mr Higgins, had collapsed in the cathedral and appeared to be in a bad way. Dr Richardson and Mr Higgins arrived just before the paramedics.

As Mr. Higgins walked down the cathedral aisle towards them, Jenny launched herself into her father's arms.

'Daddy, Daddy! Danny's collapsed on the cathedral floor! And he's cold, freezing cold.'

Danny regained consciousness in time to hear his father say:

'There there Jenny, don't worry. Everything's going to be all right, you see.'

'Good old Dad,' Danny thought. 'He might not be the coolest dad on the block but he's a tower of strength in a crisis.'

And so it seemed. Mr. Higgins tucked Jenny tightly to his side, and looking a lot paler than he did when he set out for the archive office that morning, leant over the stretcher, took Danny's hand and rubbed it between his own:

'Come on son, give us a smile.'

Danny said his first words since his arrival back into the twenty-first century: 'Hi Dad, sorry about this.' Mr Higgins then waffled on for several minutes about how Danny didn't need to say sorry and Danny knew that for once he really needed to listen carefully to his dad's words – it would help to stabilise him in the present time.

Soon, the paramedics arrived and took charge, calmly and efficiently.

'Hello,' said the first paramedic, leaning over close to Danny. 'My name's Charlie, what's yours?'

'Danny.'

'Well Danny, no need to cry.'

'I'm not,' said Danny aware that tears were running down his cheeks.

'We'll have a look at you and try to work out what's happened to you. This is Shelly, my assistant.'

'Hello Danny,' said Shelly.

'Don't worry, Danny, about crying, it's just a reaction to shock.'

Danny realised that he was crying tears of relief that he was back in the twenty-first century – back with his family. The two paramedics expertly moved Danny from the cathedral stretcher onto the one they had brought with them. Charlie took his blood pressure and temperature, while Shelly covered him with a foil blanket. Then Charlie turned round to Mr. Higgins.

'Are you his dad?'

'Yes, I am. Have you any idea why Danny collapsed?'

'We don't really know. I was hoping you might throw some light on it. To tell you the truth, we are really puzzled. But he's been unconscious so we will have to take him to A and E and a doctor fast. We can't understand why he is so cold when the temperature in the cathedral is pretty warm – after all, it's June.'

Just as Danny was being wheeled towards the West End entrance, Mum and Aunt Mabel arrived. They came through the door to be told by one of the cathedral people about the drama that had unfolded. As soon as she heard the news, Mum rushed forward to the foil-wrapped Danny.

'Danny, Oh Danny, whatever has happened?'

Danny thought for a moment of saying: 'Well Mum, SHARP really messed up and sent me back a thousand years or more, I reckon.' But fortunately he realised this would be a terrible idea. Then the memory of his mum and Aunt Mabel carrying the picnic basket drifted into his mind. He gave a suspicion of a smile:

'Have you and Aunt Mabel eaten all the sandwiches?' At this his mum didn't know whether to laugh or cry.

'Oh Danny!' was all she managed to say before Charlie and Shelly wheeled him out of cathedral and into the waiting ambulance. It set off with the siren blaring and the light flashing.

When the family arrived at the hospital, Danny had already been fast-tracked from A and E to a ward. But as he was still having tests, they were not allowed to go in to see him. They got cups of tea and went over the events of the day several times with everyone asking Jenny to tell them what she knew, over and over. Then a seemingly important doctor in a green cotton short-sleeved suit came in and introduced himself as Mr. Cameron, a consultant no less.

'We can find no broken bones or bruises of any sort. He seems mentally bright but has all the symptoms of someone suffering from exposure. We have treated him for this by trying to get his body temperature up and he is responding well. So we are mystified – but as long as your son is on the mend, that's the main thing.'

'Absolutely,' said Mr and Mrs Higgins in unison.

'We feel he should be kept in for at least another 24 hours, maybe longer, for observation.'

'Absolutely,' they both said again.

'He's receiving some medication, but we are carefully monitoring his response to this. He seems completely tired out, exhausted for some reason, and I think he needs to sleep; perhaps it would be best if you went home now and came back to see him this evening.'

'If you think that would be best.' Mr. Higgins paused. He knew his wife desperately wanted to see Danny but he turned to her and said: 'we must do what Mr Cameron recommends, dearest.'

'I suppose we must.' Mrs Higgins reluctantly agreed.

'And it won't be long until this evening, Rachel,' put in Aunt Mabel.

'You're right. Of course, you're right.'

It was a sad group that made their way back to Aunt Mabel's. When Aunt Mabel opened the front door, an excited Rocket, bounced around, giving small, excited barks, jumping up and trying to lick everyone, but nobody took much notice of him, not even Jenny. Aunt Mabel said 'On your bed Rocket!' in a sharp voice, and the dog, suddenly sensing something was wrong, slunk morosely back to his bed.

When evening visiting time came round, the ward sister beckoned to Mr. and Mrs Higgins to come into the office. She asked them lots of questions about Danny's health and whether he had had any other similar attacks. Mr and Mrs Higgins said that he was generally very healthy but there had been an occasion about nine months before when they had worried about him. He had seemed well, but was not able to pay attention to anything. The ward sister noted it all down and said that they still had no idea what had caused Danny's blackout and seemingly unaccountable loss of body heat. She told them that he had been put in a side room because he kept calling out strange and unintelligible words.

'What words?' asked Mr. Higgins.

'We couldn't make out what he was saying at all: it sounded like cheddar – does that mean anything to you?'

They all shook their heads: 'not a thing,' said Mrs Higgins.

Danny was sitting up in bed, a great broad grin across his face.

'Well, where are the grapes and chocolates that people in hospital usually get given?'

'Oh! We haven't brought any,' said Jenny.

'No, you all thought I was a goner, so why waste money on choccies!'

'Danny!' exclaimed the adults.

'I'll go and get some from the hospital shop. Can I go Mum?' said Jenny.

'No, no,' said Mum. 'Look what it says above the bed – NBM – Nil By Mouth. They all laughed and Dad and Aunt Mabel teased Danny by telling him what they had all had for tea, making the most of a rather quickly-got-together-meal of sausage and mash. It sounded heaven to Danny who was ravenous by now.

Then Jenny asked:

'What's that in your arm Danny?'

'Oh, it's a drip.' Jenny went up close and peered at the contraption and then at her brother's arm. She could see a tube inserted into the back of his hand.

'Does it hurt?'

'No, I can't even feel it.'

'I don't think I'd like it.'

'Honestly Jen, it doesn't hurt at all.'

'You gave us all a nasty shock earlier on, old man,' said Dad.

'I'm really sorry.'

'It wasn't your fault, Danny; not your fault at all.' Dad shook his head, wishing he could find someone to blame, and puzzled that the medical profession couldn't come up with a nice tidy answer to the day's events.

When it was time to leave, everyone took it in turns to give Danny a big hug. When it was Jenny's turn she said cryptically:

'Just another thing to add to the mystery surrounding my brother' – and Danny had the same feeling that he had last time he had ventured back into the past: that his sister Jenny sensed there was something he wasn't letting on about.

It was a fine sunny evening and Dad suggested

that he and Mum took Rocket for a walk while Aunt Mabel put her feet up and Jenny went to bed.

On an impulse Aunt Mabel went upstairs and found Jenny sitting up in bed crying. The day had been too much for her.

'Danny will be all right, won't he Aunt Mabel?'

'Of course he will, darling. Would you like us to ask God to take care of him?' Jenny nodded. She knew Aunt Mabel had a strong faith, and that night it made her feel safe.

'Shall we say a prayer together?'

Jenny nodded.

While the family were all having an early, restful night Danny wasn't. He found his phone in his hospital locker drawer together with a few coins, his watch, which had stopped at 12.20, his pocket book with a page headed 'Greenmen – William de Ramsey King's Master Mason'. He picked up his watch; he couldn't move the fingers and no amount of shaking would bring it to life.

CHAPTER 7

Midnight Visitors

The night sister came in to take Danny to the toilet. She had to come with him in order to wheel the drip apparatus alongside him as he walked. Danny hated having to have an adult take him for a pee. She had told him that as long as he still kept on making good progress, the drip would probably come out in the morning.

'Are we feeling sleepy?' she cooed as Danny climbed back into bed.

'Yes,' lied Danny. He wasn't feeling at all sleepy, but he didn't want any fuss, and he certainly didn't want any more unpleasant things to take.

'Well, if you want anything in the night, just press the bed button.'

'I will.'

'Good night, pet.' She closed the door quietly behind her.

It wasn't completely dark in the room, a soft overhead light meant that you could see well enough to move around but it wasn't bright enough to read.

Anyway, he hadn't got anything to read. He wished the family had brought him something, but then they had thought he was at death's door. He lay back listening to the hospital noises; a constant slight hum of some sort of equipment, the rattle of a pan in a sink and then the commotion of a trolley coming into the ward – a late night admission? He began to feel a bit drowsy. Then he saw the door handle move and the door open. He hunched down under the covers to try to convince the night sister he was well and truly asleep, so he didn't see three people come in and stand just inside the door.

'Danny,' said a voice he recognised.

Startled, Danny pushed himself up into a sitting position. The first thing he thought was that it was a dream, because just inside the room was Kaz with two other people, an older woman and a young, funky-looking girl.

'Danny, it's me Kaz.' Kaz walked forward, a finger on his lips to signal the need to be quiet. He paused for a minute and a confused, sad look flitted across his face. 'I don't know how to say this really, but we have come to apologise for what happened to you today. It was awful – really awful. We are truly sorry.'

Danny stared at Kaz and at the two others with

him. This was a deputation – SHARP had sent three people out – it will have been a massive cost – well, so it should be, after all he could have died!

'How did things go so dreadfully wrong?'asked Danny. His voice was tight, not that friendly. 'Was it a malfunction at SHARP?'

'Danny, this is Professor Aurelia Dobbs. You might remember I told you about her in our first communication.'

'I remember,' said Danny, still not being friendly in any way.

Professor Aurelia Dobbs moved closer to the hospital bed. She was only a little taller than Kaz but she was imposing, powerful and extraordinary in a way that Danny had never seen before: her hair was jet black and hung in a thick, shiny curtain around her face. She reminded Danny of an ancient Egyptian princess whose perfectly-formed features were carved on the side of tombs. Her eyes were an intense green and Danny could not stop himself looking into them. She spoke very softly, with a lilt to her voice. As he listened Danny felt as if he was being mesmerised.

'I understand completely Danny, why you are angry. Your life was in danger and your family has been upset. You were left without any secure connection to SHARP, you must have been extremely frightened.' The professor paused and looked at Danny. He could feel his anger drifting but he clung on to it – he had to let them know how he felt.

'Well, I don't mind so much about what happened to me. But I didn't want to cause all that worry to my mum and dad – and Jenny, she's only eight you know – she was crying when I was lying on the cathedral floor.'

'I know Danny, we saw it all but I want you to know it was definitely not a malfunction of SHARP systems that caused the problem The culprit is here. Phoebe, please explain to Danny.'

Aurelia Dobbs turned to the third person in the room, and motioned to the girl to come forward. As she did, Danny could clearly see that like Kaz, Professor Dobbs had six fingers and a thumb on her upheld hand.

The look that the professor gave the girl was a laser beam of anger; it seemed to physically hit Phoebe and she flinched. Danny began to feel sorry for the girl before she had even said a word.

Phoebe approached Danny's bed. Under normal circumstances, she was probably one of those cocky girls who are really irritating, but now, she struggled to get a word out. She started speaking very quietly, not looking Danny in the eye but gazing intently down at the hospital floor. Danny checked her fingers as well – Yes, seven.

'It was all my fault, Danny. I am at the student level below Kaz and I was assigned to shadow him and I'd being doing well, hadn't I Kaz?' As she asked the question, she perked up a little and Kaz nodded slightly. 'And all the other students at my level were beginning to handle the whole trip of the xrosmonauts on their own, that is without their superior student overseeing them. And I thought I should be doing the same.'

'Yes, but Phoebe, those students were all working with xrosmonauts from our time. None of them were working with twenty-first century kids. It was such an honour for you to be included in the 15798 project – you were picked especially. Danny was the first twenty-first century boy, no the first twenty-first century person to be contacted!' Kaz said the last sentence very slowly and with emphasis. 'There was just no comparison between our project and some piffling little 1522 jaunt!' Kaz was glowering at Phoebe. 'And you blew it – you totally blew it.' Danny could see that the more he spoke, the more Kaz was boiling over with anger. Goodness, Kaz was much more angry than he was!

'Look, Kaz, let Phoebe carry on explaining to me,' said Danny, because I don't really understand what it was that she did wrong. And if anyone's entitled to be cross, it's me.' Phoebe shot him a grateful look.

'What I did wrong Danny, was I continued with the project on my own on a day when Kaz had asked me to wait. I thought I was doing everything correctly. All the instruments showed that I was.'

'She thought she had sent you the mission details and that you had pressed the green button.' Kaz put in. 'But, she had not considered the outer options panel, mainly because she had never done any work on the outer options panel and they were clearly showing that you were not responding.' He turned to Phoebe and said, this time a little sadly: 'I did tell you that the outer options panel was vitally important didn't I?'

'You did Kaz, and I am very, very sorry I didn't pay more attention – I listened too much to the others.' This time Phoebe looked really sorry, almost as if she was going to start crying.

Aurelia Dobbs stepped forward. When Danny looked at her this second time, he could see that she was what twenty-first century adults would call 'stunningly beautiful' even though she was an older woman; and now she was not looking stern or fierce, in fact she was smiling gently.

'What I should explain Danny, is that, despite the enlightenment of our times, there is still jealousy and there was a great deal of jealousy amongst Kaz's fellow students because he is so gifted and because he was asked to join the 15798 project. Phoebe's friends were jealous of Kaz, and then because she joined him, jealous of her and they kept egging her on to try to outshine Kaz.

'Well, I suppose I can understand that. Dumb, but it happens. But there is one thing I would like to ask Phoebe.'

'What's that?' asked Kaz.

'What about the time/space travel bag with the disc, Phoebe? Didn't you realise that you hadn't sent the travel bag?' Before she could answer Kaz butted in:

'Oh, but she did – she did send it!' Kaz was laughing now, almost. 'She sent it to your house in Bisley! The thing about the outer options panel, Danny, to put it simply, is it lets you know if your time traveller is not at home! The whole reason Phoebe was tripped up was your visit to your relative in Lichfield

– she'd have just about got away with it if you had been at home.'

'You mean there's a travel bag in my bedroom, on the shelf next to my ridiculous elephant money-box that I daren't throw away cos my gran gave it to me?'

'Exactly, that is just where it is,' answered Kaz.

Danny started laughing as well, which made Phoebe blush a bright pink. Obviously having a twenty-first century kid laugh at her was the worst.

'And we are going to leave it there until you get home, so you know we are speaking the truth.'

'That's fine. Thanks. But… but I suppose I would also like to know how you managed to get me back?'

Suddenly everyone was serious.

'We'll not pretend Danny, that it was easy,' said Aurelia Dobbs. 'As soon as we knew there was a problem, we called in the rescue team. They have never lost a xrosmonaut yet and they were not going to let you be the first. Everyone was working at full stretch. But I must tell you, that it was you that really made the difference.'

'What do you mean?'

'You became part of the community that you found yourself in; that is what you always do so successfully, Danny. You must have connected with the people of that time in some way. They noticed you, and that gave a boost to the faint signal that was still coming from your phone, making it possible for the rescue team to lock into your co-ordinates, locate you exactly and bring you back.'

'I see.' Danny was quiet for a minute or so, remembering that he had nearly smashed his phone to the ground in desperation. And then he thought of the kindness that seemed to come from the eyes of the monk whose face he would never forget.

Professor Dobbs waited for a while, noticing Danny had gone quiet, but then she spoke very seriously.

'Danny, I must now ask you if you are prepared to carry on travelling back in time for SHARP, to undertake further work for SHARP.' Danny spotted the use of the word 'work'; they had never used that word before.

'I don't know. If it was just me, I'd be fine with it but you know, what happened was really hard on Mum and Dad.'

'We know that, we do indeed and we will try to make it up to them,' said Professor Dobbs

'How?'

'I am sure we will be able to find a way.'

'Well OK, but I think you could be a bit more straight with me.'

'What do you mean, Danny?' asked Kaz.

'This whole thing isn't just about gathering information about the past is it?'

'You see,' laughed Kaz, 'I told you Danny would begin to ask questions – want to know more.'

'Alright, alright Kaz, stop crowing,' said Professor Dobbs. 'You are right Danny, it isn't all about gathering information about the past. The fact is, it is much more serious than that. It's about keeping the world, the earth, humankind in existence – keeping civilisation and the very planet we all live on, from being destroyed.' She paused. 'Is that what you wanted to hear?'

'I don't know – maybe. But I don't understand.'

'I would need a long, long time to explain fully, Danny. And I wouldn't want to insult your intelligence by saying 'you won't understand' but it involves very complex scientific knowledge some of which was not even touched upon in your time, although it was the massive increase in the use of computers that led to our eventual discoveries about the nature of time. But if I can say to you this: everything that is recorded in a human mind, leaves a trace. Just as everything that is stored on a computer leaves a trace and can be retrieved by someone who knows how, so everything that has happened that has been recorded in a human mind, leaves behind a trace; every kind action, every cruel action leaves a trace. But the trace left by cruel actions can be used by certain beings, (they are not people in the real sense of the word although they might have begun their existence as people) for very dreadful purposes. These forces try to bring about total destruction, and so in the twentieth century, there were wars that became ever more terrible. We humankind in the future are constantly fighting to overcome destruction, not just for our time, but for your time as well. That is the whole purpose of SHARP.' Aurelia Dobbs looked at Danny to see how her words were affecting him. Despite her aura of power, Danny looked steadily into her eyes.

'Yes Danny, your trips back into the past are not just information-gathering jaunts, although that is an important function, we have not lied to you there. The disc you wear not only shows us what is happening at that time but it enables us to see the traces that have been left and that is very helpful to us.'

For a moment Danny was silent. This was way more than he had bargained for.

'But surely, isn't that interfering with the course of history?' he asked.

'No, not at all Danny,' said Kaz. 'It's the trace that we look at, that's all: the trace left by evil that leads to the future, not to the present.'

'Well, if you say so. It all sounds a bit serious, and I can't say I really understand it, but...,' Danny shrugged... 'it sounds like it's all in a good cause.' He gave a nervous grin.

Kaz grinned back. 'Exactly – are you in?'

'Could you doubt it?' said Danny.

Aurelia Dobbs leant forward and gave Danny a small but formal handshake, using the hand that was not attached to the drip.

'Thank you,' she said.

'Does that mean I'm forgiven?' asked Phoebe.

'Only if you never touch one of my trips again,' said Danny laughing. 'Well, not until you've grasped the principles of the outer options, anyway.'

'She won't. It will definitely be me that's your contact from our end.' Kaz said. The three visitors turned to go.

'Wait a minute,' Danny called.

'What is it?' asked Kaz.

'I don't even know what year it was I went back

to and where – was it Lichfield?'

'Oh yes, it was Lichfield alright. It was Lichfield in the Year 671 and the place where you were, is where they built the holy shrine that later became the site of the cathedral.'

'Woah – cool totally cool.'

'See you Danny.' Kaz gave the thumbs up sign.

'Goodbye Danny,' said Aurelia Dobbs and Phoebe.

'Goodbye,' said Danny.

After they left, Danny fell asleep in two minutes flat.

When Danny woke up in the morning, the first thing he thought about was breakfast – food. He was ravenously hungry but then the next thought he had, was that he needed to pee. He lay in bed squirming with the embarrassing thought that he would have to ring and get someone to come with him to the toilet. He hung on as long as possible and then rang the bell. A girl came who looked about sixteen.

'Good morning,' she said with a bright smile. 'What is it?'

'Is the night sister still on, the one who was here

last night?'

'Course not, she'll be home having her tea by now – everything's back to front for them. Anyway didn't you hear me say 'good morning'?

'Yes.' Danny wondered if he could hold on. He couldn't go to the toilet with this girl!

'What was it you wanted?'

'Oh nothing.'

'Well why did you ring the bell?' She looked at him and grinned. 'You want to go to the toilet don't you?' Danny didn't say anything. 'It's OK I won't look –promise and anyway I'm a nurse. Come on stop making a fuss.'

They went to the toilet and she was as good as her word: she didn't look. On their way back Danny could see down into the main ward. There were children who obviously were very poorly, like the small boy propped up on a pile of pillows, with a very white face and no hair. Had he had to have that treatment for cancer that made your hair fall out? It made Danny feel like a fraud.

'I'm awfully hungry,' he said to the young nurse. 'Can I have some breakfast?'

'Well, I don't know – it says NBM. I'll go and ask sister.' She didn't come back and no breakfast appeared. Time dragged. Then suddenly Mr. Cameron appeared with a group of medical students, all armed with clipboards.

'Good morning Danny.'

'Good morning Mr. Cameron.'

'This is Danny Higgins, who collapsed yesterday in Lichfield Cathedral and has shown all the signs of hypothermia – Now…' he peered round the group selecting a victim, 'Miss Clark, what do you think could be the cause?'

'Could he have had some sort of fit?' offered Miss Clark

'He could have done, but he didn't. Any other thoughts?'

'He'd just come back from the Antarctic?' a joker's voice from the back put in. There were a few muffled chuckles.

'If that is the level of diagnosis from this group – we are in serious trouble.' Mr. Cameron was not amused. 'I want you all to go away and think carefully about this case, take all the test results into consideration and write a report for me by the end of the day.' Mr. Cameron then turned towards his patient and in quite a different tone of voice said: 'Is there anything you'd like to tell me Danny?'

'Yes, I haven't eaten anything since breakfast yesterday and I'm starving.'

'Well that's a good sign. Sister would you get someone to bring some toast for this young man?' The consultant with his flock of students moved on.

Two rounds of toast and a cup of hot chocolate were brought to him by a ward assistant. Nothing had ever tasted so good!

Boredom was setting in seriously, when a large V-shaped mop suddenly appeared round the door, closely followed by a large square-shaped cleaning woman. She whizzed the mop round his bed and with a great flourish swished it underneath, and then the mop and its operator were out the door. A moment later she re-appeared; this time with a small trolley that held a bowl of water and an assortment of cloths, sponges and cleaning sprays. With a splash here, a spray there and a quick rub, she had done the surfaces and was on her way out when she paused, fished a notepad and pencil from her pocket and turned to Danny and said:

'And what were yer wanting for yer dinner?'

Dinner, my goodness dinner! Here were the best words he'd heard all morning.

'What's on offer?'

'What's on offer? Yer cheeky lad. It's poy, baked taters, gravy an stewed apple puddin and custard. Or…' a long pause the pencil poised strategically over the pad, while she looked at Danny as if he were a newly-discovered specimen '…there's the salad option. That's tuna.'

'I'll have the poy, I mean pie.'

She made a small mark on her pad, stuck it back in her pocket and was away.

Later that afternoon, Danny was declared well enough to go home. The drip had been taken out before lunch and the results from the tests had come back, all indicating that Danny was fit and well. His mother, hardly able to believe that the dreadful shock was over, had brought his clothes: Danny's stay in hospital was at an end. Before they left, Mrs Higgins insisted that Danny went and thanked the nursing staff for their care. Feeling a little wobbly on his legs from being in bed for twenty-four hours, Danny took it slowly across the hospital car park.

'You know mum, there were some really sick kids on that ward.'

'I know, Danny – I'm just grateful you're not one of them.'

CHAPTER 8

Calm Waters And A Bit Of Exaggeration

Leaning over the side of a narrow boat, listening to the quiet chug of the diesel engine on a warm summer's day was, Danny thought, not the most exciting activity, but it was a great way to get rid of memories of nearly freezing to death. He was so happy to be back in the ordinary world of everyday life. This was the last day of their stay with their aunt and she had suggested a trip to the marina as a way of making the most of it. It was pretty obvious that his mum had thought it a good way to entertain, but not too taxing for Danny, still recovering from what his family now referred to as his 'mystery' illness.

The sun was shining, the narrow boat people were jolly and everyone seemed to be enjoying themselves. There were two crew and about twenty passengers. He watched his mum with Jenny on the other side of the boat, looking for animal holes in the mud of the canal bank. Is that where ratty lived, the loveable character from Wind in the Willows? Or could it possibly be the home of an otter? Funny how people found water rats lovable, but land rats were so hated. Then, for a moment the pack of wolves, their jaws gaping, flashed back unasked into Danny's mind. He gave a shiver and went over to sit beside his aunt.

'Look, Danny we're just approaching a lock,' she said. 'Do you know how they work?'

'No, I don't really, Aunt Mabel. I know you have them on canals, but I don't know why – what are they for? Are they to stop boats going too fast?'

'Don't be silly,' laughed Aunt Mabel. 'The locks make the canals navigable – they stop the water not the boats going too fast, if you like. Watch what happens when we go through this lock that's coming up now and you'll get the idea.'

As they approached a lock, Jenny came over to join them and they watched together as a member of the crew jumped out onto the towpath and walked up to the lock. They could see the young chap put his full weight behind the long arm of the gate to slowly open it; then he had to walk across the gate at the top to get to the other side and do the same, so that both gates were far enough back to let them in. The boat chugged into the small space between the front and back gates and the one behind closed. The crew member then starting turning the mechanism to let the water out of the lock. The boat went down and down about eight feet, as the water level dropped. The enclosed space between the two gates now seemed like a large well; the dank brick-built sides dripped water and green slime. Then gates at the other end of the lock opened; the water in the lock was now equal to that of the canal on this side and the boat could continue on its way downstream.

'I see,' said Danny. 'It's like we have come down a step – that's clever.'

'It is, especially when you think how long ago the canals were built,' Aunt Mabel said.

'When was that?' asked Jenny.

'Oh, I don't know exactly probably nearly two hundred years ago, I should think; early Victorian.'

Mum went to ask the man in charge if Jenny and Danny could help at the next lock. He nodded and grinned:

'Always ready to use some unpaid boat hands. But they must be sensible and not run or anything – Health and Safety you know.'

So at the next lock, Jenny and Danny scrambled out on to the towpath and walked up to help push one of the huge wooden arms back, to open the gates. They were amazed at how heavy it was. They were told to keep well away from the sides, but as the water started draining out, they couldn't resist peering over at the boat dropping slowly down into the lock well.

'Mum's still worrying about you,' said Jenny.

'Yup, I know, she's probably expecting me to keel over at any time! I bet she's stressing right now that I might collapse and fall into the lock!'

That was exactly what Mrs Higgins was doing. Aunt Mabel could see from her face that her niece was imagining the worst.

'You mustn't worry about him Rachel. He looks fine now – colour in his cheeks and he's almost back to his old lively self.'

'I know, but look up there at him – if he collapsed like he did in the cathedral, he would just tipple over into the lock!'

'Rachel!'

'Oh I am sorry, I must make an effort to get over it – well, it was just so odd.'

'I know, but really the best thing for Danny is to let him forget it and not try and wrap him up in cotton wool.'

'You're right, Aunt Mabel – You're always right. And anyway, now I should be worrying about you.'

'You don't need to Rachel – you know I've been very lucky with my health so far, so getting a bit of heart trouble at my age is not so surprising.'

'Let me know how the tests go.'

'I will and don't you and the family stay away so long this time.'

Later in the afternoon, drinks, tea and cake were given out and the captain once more asked for 'unpaid hands' to help pass these out from the small galley below, to the passengers sitting on the rows of benches, that filled the space where once there would have been the cargo of coal or china clay for the potteries. Danny and Jenny happily helped out.

When they got home, there was a message on Aunt Mabel's answerphone: Dad was going to be late; he and Dr Richardson were going to a pub just outside Lichfield for a drink and a bite to eat on their last evening. They would come back after that. They got in about nine o'clock just as Jenny and Danny were going to bed. Dr Richardson was a tall, jolly man full of guffaws, teasing Danny about his collapse in the cathedral.

'You wouldn't be the first to be lying unconscious on the cathedral stones,' he said.

'Wouldn't I?' asked Danny.

'There was many a soldier lying on the floor at the time of the siege, fatally wounded by gunshot or sword.'

'When was that?' asked Danny.

'When the Lord Brooke was attacking the Royalists who were barricaded in the Close; defending the cathedral from the Parliamentarians.'

'That's the time of the Civil War?'

'That's it Danny. Lord Brooke was one who had joined the new faith and he believed that the cathedral and other great religious buildings like it stood for all that was wrong in the old faith. He wanted to destroy it. You can read all about it in this book I've brought you – just a second-hand copy you understand, 'A Brief History of Lichfield Cathedral.'

'Thank you very much Dr Richardson,' said Danny.

'That's very kind of you,' said Rachel Higgins.

'Oh, not at all. And I brought this for our young artist. It's a little book of sketches of Lichfield and its famous sons.'

'Thank you Dr Richardson,' said Jenny, turning over the pages with interest.

Not many eight-year-old girls would be so pleased with such a book, thought the doctor. What an interesting family they were! He shook hands with everyone and called out to Aunt Mabel as he left:

'See you at the next U3A history lecture, Mabel.'

Next day, as usual, Danny was packed up ready to go about an hour before everyone else, while Jenny, Mum and Dad dashed around picking up their sundry belongings from all sorts of corners in Aunt Mabel's rambling house.

'You'll no doubt have to send on something someone's left behind,' he remarked to Aunt Mabel.

'Well, not everyone can be so obsessively tidy as you Danny,' she teased. 'You know I'm not so tidy myself.'

'That's true,' Danny said and then: 'Ooo...er sorry Aunt Mabel.'

'Well, no need to be. You're right Danny. So I think you must be the odd one out in the family.'

'I think I must be.'

They all drove away a little sad that it would be the last visit to the big old house, and Jenny waved frantically at the disappearing figure of Aunt Mabel holding Rocket in her arms, until they turned out of the street and couldn't see her anymore.

When they got home, Danny dashed upstairs

with his backpack. And, yes, the space/time travel bag was on his shelf, just as Kaz had said it would be. He opened it and saw that the round disc was inside. He picked up the disc and examined it carefully. He'd never really had time to do that before. It was slightly flexible but clearly made of something very tough. The black backing was very shiny but thinner than the see-through part at the front – that was probably as much as two or three millimetres thick. That was the part that adhered to the forehead and then seemed to dissolve into it, when you pressed the black backing against your skin. Danny put the disc back into the bag and then put the bag back on the shelf where it had been, next to the elephant-shaped moneybox. When he looked the next day, it had gone.

Walking to school with Mark on the first morning back, Danny knew that he was in for non-stop reporting on Mark's doings in the 'US of A' as he called it, and that it might go on for several days, maybe even weeks – not that Mark was good at describing things, owing to his rather limited use of the English language, but that wouldn't stop him repeating the names of places and saying things like 'WOW' and 'WICKED'. Danny had already counted ten 'wickeds' and they hadn't even got out of Disneyland.

At lunch-break, they were joined by Steve and Griff who hung on Mark's every word, so in awe were they, of anyone who had travelled so much in the States. Their main comments were 'awesome!'

'Disneyland was great, but you know I've been there before and it's kind of a bit for small kids you know, although there are some wicked rides,' (eleven counted Danny) 'but I much preferred Las Vegas. Have you ever been to Las Vegas?' Of course, all of his three friends shook their heads.

'My uncle's been and he won some money on the one-armed bandits.' Steve tried to get some reflected glory from his uncle's visit but nobody was interested.

'WOW, that place is just wicked.' (Danny notched up number twelve.) 'The hotel we stayed in was huge – it was all done on a jungle theme, there were real lions and tigers.

'Any wolves?' asked Danny.

'No,' Mark looked a bit puzzled.

'The swimming pool was massive and it was really like being in a jungle. There were vines and ropes and monkeys up in the ceiling and everything.' Mark carried on listing the wonders of Las Vegas and just got in about a helicopter ride to see the Grand Canyon, which Danny thought really would have been 'wicked' before the bell went. As they ran back to lessons, Danny wondered whether he should tell Mark his 'wicked' score – it was up to twenty – but then thought better of it; he'll only say, I'm being 'compulsive' he thought, which he probably was.

On the way home, Mark continued with his account of the States but then remembered that he hadn't asked Danny anything about his holiday week.

'Where did you go?'

'We went to Lichfield to visit Mum's aunt – there's some cool places to go round there, Drayton Manor theme park had some…'Danny paused and then said with a wry smile… 'wicked rides.'

'Oh yeah? But, Danny you should have seen the sports shops out there in the US of A.. They had every type of gear you could imagine. And in one of the hotels we stayed at, they taught you baseball. I got kitted out properly and had a go – it's a really awesome game. Sorry, Danny what was it you were saying about your hols – you went to visit your aunt?'

'Yes,' said Danny – he could understand Mark's lack of interest but he couldn't help feeling a stab of annoyance. He suddenly thought he might wind Mark up a bit and go for the sympathy vote big time. 'Well, you see, Dad had to talk to a chap at the archive office so Jenny and I were dropped off at the cathedral. Jenny wanted to do some drawing and I was searching for green men.'

'Oh yeah,' said Mark, not even trying to disguise his obvious boredom.

Undeterred, Danny went on, 'You'll never guess what happened in the cathedral...'

'The bells rang, the choir sang?'

'No, not even close,' said Danny.

'Oh the bishop said some rude words in the pulpit?'

'No,' said Danny.

'I give up,' said Mark.

'I began to feel quite queasy, and giddy.'

'I know, I know,' said Mark 'you puked all over the bishop.'

'No stupid, the bishop wasn't even in the cathedral. I collapsed – I became totally unconscious and paramedics couldn't revive me so an ambulance took me to the nearest hospital where a team of doctors couldn't do anything for me. By the way I was still unconscious at this stage.' Danny was getting into the swing of things and he could see he was having quite an effect on Mark. Hospitals were the one thing that managed to send shivers down Mark's back. He had a dread of hospitals, and injections in particular.

'What happened then, when the doctors couldn't get you round?'

'I don't know, do I?' said Danny. 'But I do remember, when I did come round. I had tubes feeding something into my arm. It looked like a big upside down bottle of lemonade with a tube from it that went into the back of my hand. It was all taped up with surgical tape. It's a good job I haven't got hairy hands, as it would have been agony when they tore it off and pulled the tube out of my vein.'

At this Mark pulled a face and stuck his tongue out as if he was going to be sick.

Danny was really enjoying things now.

'I was NBM.'

'What's that?'

'Nil by mouth. I was by this time, feeling very cold despite the blankets and hot water bottles they put in my bed. The really unpleasant bit was all the injections I had to have.' ('All' was actually three in total.)

'They were really painful.'

'Oh – I hate injections. Don't tell me any more!'

'Well if I hadn't had them, I might not have come round.'

'You didn't ... Mark hesitated, 'you didn't actually cry did you?'

'No I didn't' Danny said indignantly, 'but I felt close to it mind you. And whilst you were stuffing your face with doughnuts and every kind of treat, I was NBM.'

'Nil by mouth,' repeated Mark.

'When I was allowed food, the first thing I had was toast – it tasted amazing, I can tell you. At first, my visitors weren't allowed to bring grapes, chocolate, fruit or anything like that.'

'Well, what was actually wrong with you?'

'They said I had all the symptoms of HYPOTHERMIA.' (Danny was pretty sure Mark wouldn't know what that was.)

'Hypothermia – isn't that the thing mountaineers get when they are   stranded on the mountainside on very, very cold nights?'

'Yes.' Now it was Danny's turn to look impressed – fancy Mark knowing what hypothermia was.

'So they thought you caught hypothermia in Lichfield Cathedral in June?'

'Yeah, I told you it was odd. I had to have loads of tests.'

'What tests?'

'Oh blood tests – it's a wonder I have any blood left; they tested for liver function, kidney function and iron.'

'How do they do that?'

'They put a band around your arm above the elbow to make your veins stand out and then slide (Danny emphasised the word 'slide' watching Mark get more and more uncomfortable) a needle in and draw the blood out slowly. They put the blood into different tubes with various coloured tops.'

Poor Mark was looking decidedly pale. Danny rolled up his sleeve and there were the outlines of bruises turned a rather disgusting yellowy-purple colour.

'Oh, how awful. Gosh, will the hypothermia thingy come back?'

'I don't know,' said Danny, 'but I really, really hope not. I never want to go through that again.' Danny rolled his sleeve down. They walked on in silence for a while and Danny suddenly began to worry that he had somewhat overdone things.

'I say Mark, don't mention any of this to the others will you? You know Griff and Steve. I don't want people to think that I'm some sort of …you know … invalid or whatever.'

'No mate, of course not.'

'I bet your Mum and Dad were out of their minds with worry.'

'They were; Aunt Mabel and Jenny as well. Anyhow mate, I'm absolutely fine now – no problems at all – see yer tomrrow.'

'See yer Danny.'

That evening Danny told Jenny about the faces Mark pulled when he told him about the drip and having blood tests.

'Oh Jen, I really thought he was going to be sick, there and then on the pavement.'

'I bet you exaggerated.'

'Of course I didn't – well yes just a bit – maybe a lot actually but it was such fun.'

'Poor Mark. I bet he's one of those people who are really squeamish about injections.'

'Oh yes, oh yes he is.'

'Well it wasn't very kind then was it?'

'No, but it was fun. Besides, I'd had a whole day of the US of A.'

'The what? That's what Mark's dad calls the United States.'

It all backfired on Danny rather, because later that evening his mum came and said:

'Danny, what on earth have you been telling Mark?' She had just been an hour on the phone to Helen, Mark's mum explaining that Danny's condition was not serious; yes it was unexplained, no he wasn't having any treatment, yes he was perfectly fine now.

'The thing ended up, Danny,' his mum explained, 'with Helen saying that she and Ron were hoping that you might have a week away with them this August at one of those Centre Park places they go to so much.

They're finding that Mark gets a bit bored because he's on his own and sometimes it is hard to make new friends in such a short while. They were going to contact us this weekend to find out if we would be happy with that, and they even wondered if Jenny would like to come along as well.'

'Can I? Can I?' begged Jenny.

'So what did you say?' asked Danny.

'Well, of course I said I would talk it over with your dad and you and let her know as soon as possible. They'd have to book pretty soon. It would be a good break in the holidays because I'm not at all sure we can afford to get away this summer. I really want to use all our savings for the extension. Would you like to go?'

'Yes, if my failing health allows it.' Danny put a hand to his forehead and swooned on to the sofa.

'Danny! That's not funny! I know perfectly well what happened. When you told Mark about Lichfield, he probably wasn't in the least interested so you made your hospital visit sound as gruesome as possible, didn't you?'

CHAPTER 9

Another Trip To Lichfield

One Friday evening, about five weeks after their return from Lichfield, Danny was sitting at his computer doing his homework – getting it out of the way so he would have the weekend free. It was Griff's birthday and they were all going bowling on Saturday. He'd almost finished his maths and still had English to do when he felt it – the pulse from his phone that indicated that someone from SHARP was getting in touch.

He pushed his chair back, stood up and breathed in deeply, to stop himself feeling too excited. He pressed the black button and as usual the screen slid away from the mobile and expanded to the size of a TV screen, floating just in front of him.

Hi Danny, it's me Kaz, definitely me! Can we communicate on your computer? It's better than the phone because you can type replies back to me. Switch your phone off and just come out of the document you're in – is it your homework?

Leave your screen saver on then our screen will come up.

Danny switched his phone off and followed Kaz's instructions; the same intense blue screen that was on his mobile, filled his desktop. For a few seconds there were no words, just swirling colours and then the screen filled up with text.

Hi again. I'd like to say it was great to see you in the hospital, but it wasn't, of course, because of the reason you were there – that stupid Phoebe girl! You were pretty amazing, though Danny. Professor Dobbs was extremely impressed that you weren't hard on Phoebe.

What's happened to Phoebe?

Oh she's got to go back and repeat the whole first part of her course. She's pretty fed up but she's lucky she didn't get thrown out altogether. The only thing is, once a person's made such a big mistake, they can improve a lot because they'll never do that kind of thing again. What did you think of Professor Dobbs?

Oh my goodness – she was the most scary person I have ever met – I mean I've never, never met anyone like her.

She is absolutely tops in her field – unbelievably clever, but I know what you mean, scary as well. If you hadn't forgiven Phoebe, she would have had no hesitation in banishing her.

Banishing her?

Oh that's just SHARP talk for being thrown out of SHARP. But, no more gossiping – I've got to get the information to you about your next trip. You'll notice some differences in the instructions. Do you remember what Aurelia Dobbs told you about the additional purposes of your travels back in time?

I'm not likely to have forgotten. I mean stuff like saving the world from destruction, is kind of memorable.

Well, you can probably guess that because we

want to pick up the traces of bad actions: cru-
elty, evil, call it what you will, (we call them fracs
actually; short for fractures) that you are more
likely now to be placed in situations that might
seem dangerous.

Not like my first two trips. Were they sort of trial
runs?

Exactly – no danger, or very little. That's not the
case anymore but you don't need to worry. You
will still be safe because we have devised a protection shield that activates automatically in the
event of anything like a bullet or bomb going off
near you.

Sounds a bit like an airbag in a car.

Could be, though I'm not familiar with airbags; I
don't really know a lot about your cars at all. I
think I'd really like to drive one, though; in fact I'd
love to get behind the wheel of one of your cars!

Don't you have cars in your time?

There are other means of travel, and we don't get around as much as you do, I can tell you that – no cars. But to get back to what I was telling you; the protection shield means that you can't be injured by a bullet, and there will be some bullets whizzing about where you are going. Because of the seriousness of the situation, we would like you to read up a bit about the time you are going back to, just so as you know something about what's going on, and, of course, the place. Are you OK with that?

I'll give it a go.

The time is 1643 and the place is Lichfield Cathedral.

I was kind of guessing it was going to be Lichfield.

Yeah, I thought you might. An unusual place, small but lots of historic connections. Do you know of a time in the next week or so when it would be a good time for you to go – when you might be on your own?

For how long?

A bit longer than usual; about thirty minutes your time; getting on for a day in the time you're visiting.

Jenny's got a parents' evening next week – I think it's Wednesday but I'm not sure. I could text you later this evening?

Great. Thanks Danny. I'll say goodbye now. But text me that date.

Bye Kaz, I will.

Danny sat thinking about the new messages he had received for quite some minutes and then went and got the book Dr Richardson had given him, 'A Brief History of Lichfield Cathedral' – how useful. He opened it and started to read, homework forgotten. When he went down for tea he said casually to Jenny:

'Is it your parents' evening next week? What evening is it?'

'It's next Wednesday, why?'

'I was just wondering – have Mum and Dad promised you anything if you've done well?'

'They haven't said anything yet.'

'They will, Jen, they will. They always do.'

'I'd really like a new pair of trainers.'

'I'm betting a substantial bet that you'll get them.'

'Why – do you think I'll get a good report? For all you know I might have spent the year messing about. So what are you betting me?'

'An extra large Snickers.'

Jenny grinned – she did have a bit of a sweet tooth: 'you're on.'

Danny fished his mobile out and sent the text message, 'Next Wed. House empty 18.00 hrs.' 'Looks like a spy communicating with base', he thought and that was what he felt like sometimes: a spy operating under cover so that not even his family knew what he was up to.

On Wednesday, when school finished, Danny avoided Mark and Steve, who were expecting him to go down to the nets for some batting practice. He could have gone, he had plenty of time but he knew he wouldn't be able to concentrate; he was wound up tight as a spring – a mixture of excitement and fear had been boiling and bubbling away below the surface all day, so he'd found it hard to get through a day of double science, geography and RE. And, as well, after the hospital fiasco and Mum and Dad being given all that worry, there was a niggling feeling of guilt – guilt at not being straight with everyone.

For weeks now, he had been playing over in his mind the words that Aurelia Dobbs had said to him in the hospital and he knew without a shadow of doubt that he would not refuse to co-operate with SHARP, but the most difficult thing, was not being able to tell anyone. It wasn't as if he was just going on an adventure for adventure's sake, although there was no denying it, he loved the risk, the excitement, the thought that he was doing something not even the richest person in the world could do – yes, that was all great. But maybe he wouldn't take the risk, if that intimidating professor from the future hadn't explained that he was helping to prevent something so massive, so mind-bogglingly huge as the destruction of the world.

It was, Danny sometimes thought, almost as if he had been programmed to be the boy to take part in SHARP's activities: his parents and their parents before them were anti-war, pacifists; his mum and dad had gone with a group down to London to protest against Tony Blair joining America in the Iraq war; he'd never been allowed to play with guns, even as a toddler. Also, he was almost certain that a cousin or something of his great-granddad on Dad's side had been court-martialled and shot for not joining the army in the First World War. So, he reasoned if his Mum and Dad did know that he was helping, in whatever inexplicable way, to lessen the likelihood of future wars, surely they would approve?

The strange thing was though, despite the conviction of his parents, he'd never really got round to thinking what his own ideas were about war. It was so easy to see pictures on the telly of people being blown up, badly injured or dead and then just forget about it – go and have your tea or something. The computer games he really liked playing with Mark were the war games, and he remembered the time when he had teased Mum and Dad by saying that he might join the army when he grew up. They were truly shocked, and it was all he could do to convince them that he was just joking. In reality he had no idea at all what he wanted to do for a career.

When he got home, his mum greeted him with:

'Oh good, you're home nice and early. Will you go round to the Co-op and get me some things I need for tea?' she waved a list at him and the re-useable carrier bag. Danny took them both from her a bit impatiently; he had so wanted to go upstairs and see if the time/space travel bag had arrived. He dashed to the shop, bought the things on the list and was just about to dash back, when he remembered something: better get Jenny's Snickers bar – there's no way Jen won't get a good report.

'I've loads of homework, Mum,' he called as he escaped upstairs. He went straight to his shelf and there, next to the elephant money-box was the travel bag. It looked strangely fatter than usual. 'Hmm..odd,' he thought, but decided not to open it just in case someone came in. He got out his school-books and put them by the computer, but there was no way he could look at them.

He paced up and down the room a little and then picked up his copy of 'A Brief History of Lichfield Cathedral'. During the weekend, he had read how in 1643, the year he was to go back to, the town was besieged by Cromwell's supporters; they were called the Parliamentarians. Royalists who were for the King, defended the town. The cathedral, it seemed had been used more like a castle than a place of worship with soldiers firing from the roof on the invaders below.

What he couldn't understand was how the townspeople lived through it all. There was a passage he had read over and over again to try and make sense of it:

'Edward Peyto commanding the Parliamentarians had given the order for his soldiers to hunt down the families, the wives and children of Royalist soldiers who lived in the Close of Lichfield. Under normal circumstances this would have been a difficult task because neighbours would have been protective. But in the conditions prevailing at the time, neighbour betrayed neighbour and even families, brother and brother, father and son could be on different sides and so betray one another. Any household that appeared not to have a man in it, was under suspicion and the women and children were rounded up and held captive.'

What the book didn't explain clearly was what happened to the women and children after that. But that passage made him hope very much that if he ended up in the thick of the battle (after all Kaz had said there would be bullets flying around), he would find himself with the Royalists. The thing was though, he found it completely impossible to relate what he was reading about in the book to the quiet Cathedral Close he had visited a month or two ago.

At last Dad came in from work. He was a bit later than usual so there was a great deal of banging about and bustling going on. Danny nipped downstairs and started helping his mum put the things on the table for tea. The family sat down to a tuna and egg salad. After what seemed like an excruciating amount of time, it was 18.00 hours and Mum, Dad and Jenny left for the parents' evening. There was going to be an event in the hall afterwards with the school choir to which Jenny belonged and the orchestra performing, so Danny knew they wouldn't be back for at least a couple of hours. Phewww!

With his foot on the bottom stair, his phone began to pulse with the now familiar SHARP signal. At the same time, the hall phone rang. He picked it up to find that it was a cold call from a double-glazing firm. Putting the receiver down, he suddenly had a thought; supposing Mum and Dad rang to check how he was? That was quite a possibility since his hospital stay. They were often giving him little sideways looks to see if he was still upright! Hmm... best to leave the receiver askew, that way it would give an engaged signal and then when they came home they would think that the last person had just not put it back carefully enough. He congratulated himself on this idea – he was definitely acquiring counter-intelligence skills – perhaps spying might be his career path?

Once inside the bathroom, he locked the door behind him, just in case. He pressed the black button. The screen floated away and SHARP instructions appeared:

<Details of Current Travel Option>

<Time Zone>
March 1643.

<Place>
Midlands, England – City of Lichfield.

<Landing>
Outside the wall of the cathedral.

<Instructions>
Put on the breeches in the time/space travel bag before leaving; we are prepared for the extra power this will entail. There will be clothes on a bush near a horse trough where young lads have been washing. Join any of them who are there at the same time as you.

<Destination>

Inside the Cathedral.

<Conditions>

A bright March day, not too cold, no pestilence.
There is a battle about to start. There will be
danger but the protective shield will be in place.
You must not take a combatant role even
though you may be asked. Time to leave if that
happens.

<Identity>

Daniel Bagot – known as the Bagot boy – dis-
tantly connected to wealthy landowner – friend
of local lad Erik Christianson.

<Equipment>

Mobile phone. Travel bag with recording disc inside. Mobile phone fitted with beam of light.

If you decide to take up this travel option, do as
follows:

> Take off your clothes, except for underpants
    and put on the breeches that are in the bag.
    Do not tie the tapes.

> Press the time/space travel bag to your

body, underneath the breeches

> Key in 15798

> Press the green button.

Good luck with this advanced trip.

As he had always done, Danny read and re-read the instructions and smiled slightly to see that in 1643 his name was to be 'Daniel'. He noticed as well that in the last sentence the word 'advanced' was used. It gave him a slight churning in his stomach – this was not going to be a picnic. He followed the instructions carefully and without giving himself a moment to consider, dialled 15798 and pressed the green button. As always, he heard the faint high-pitched whine come closer and closer. He just had time to remember how shocking it was when he had heard it in the cathedral with no forewarning and then…Nothing.

CHAPTER 10

The Roof

Danny landed with what appeared to be a bump, but wasn't; it was the shock of having nothing under him and then there being something – hard earth. Every time he had gone back into the past he had experienced the same sensation, except of course, on the Phoebe trip.

He was sitting on some scruffy grass, close to a high wall. In front of him, with their backs to him, which is why they had not spotted his sudden arrival, three lads were doing a lot of splashing in a horse trough. They were flicking water and laughing while one of them seemed intent on frothing up an extremely hard lump of soap. Obviously it was the morning scrub up.

Despite feeling unpleasantly wobbly, Danny scrambled to his feet. Trying hard to focus his mind, he took in a deep breath. The air smelt strangely of cordite, like bonfire night. Although there was a fitful sun peering out between clouds, it was quite chilly. Keeping his eye on the lads at the water trough, he quickly slipped his mobile into the travel bag that was securely stuck to his middle and just about hidden by the breeches. He took out the black shiny disc and pressed it to his forehead. He felt the clear surface stick to his skin and come away from the backing. He put the backing disc into the bag and wiped his hand across his forehead. As always the disc appeared to have melted into his skin. He knew that now everything he was seeing and hearing was being relayed back to SHARP.

He made a quick check to make sure the bag was closed securely and hidden by the pants, and then walked towards the water trough. He was still feeling very peculiar as if he was not really there: a feeling he now recognised all too clearly as 'time slip' – he'd had it on the outward and the return with both of his first two journeys back in time. He plunged his arms in the trough up to his elbows. The water was freezing. That made him focus all right!

'Hey, Bagot – you look as if you've had a wash already!' shouted one lad, a tall chap with a shock of blond tousled hair. 'Hmm,' thought Danny, 'if I didn't wash for a month, I'd probably still be cleaner than you lot.'

'Aye, I have.' Danny took his arms out of the

water and shook them over the backs of the three still washing. This led to howls of mock rage and an attempt, a half-hearted attempt, by the three of them to catch him as he dodged and swerved out of their way. Suddenly one stood still and said:

'We mustn't waste our energy on larks, there's serious work to do today.'

'Aye,' the other two murmured and an anxious silence settled on them.

Danny was trying to locate which of the piles of clothes that were scattered on the grass, were his. All four looked much the same, and then he saw that one lot were piled on a bush: those were his. He started pulling up a pair of white woollen socks, glad that they were quite warm. He realised that the ties that hung from the bottom of the breeches went over the socks and kept them up. There was a clean (well sort of clean) white shirt, quite thick and made of linen and a rather shabby padded waistcoat. Danny, having to work out how to fasten everything up, was taking much longer than the other three getting dressed, and two of them left, hurrying up a path towards the sound of the hubbub. The blond lad came up to Danny as he was pushing his feet into the black leather shoes.

'Yer don't half take a long time dressing – just like

a girl,' he teased, dodging to one side, as if Danny was going to bop him. Danny held up his fists to show he was up for a playful fight.

'Ah…come on, as Sam Smith said, there's much to be done today, and no time for messing about.' The lad, who Danny thought must be Erik Christianson, set off up the path, and Danny followed. Very soon, they came into a space where a great many people were milling about and Danny lost sight of his guide. The high walls of the cathedral towered above them; Danny could tell it was Lichfield because of the three spires, but he hardly recognised the quiet, dignified Close he had visited with his family. The jumble of houses clustered around the cathedral walls entirely changed the outlook. Many of the houses were small, mean dwellings, not much more than hovels; others were grander with wide, bowed windows and tall front doors. Danny pushed his way through the throng of people to get a better view and there in front of him was a huge gate and beyond that a drawbridge. There must be a moat, the other side of that wall, Danny thought. It was more as if he was standing by a castle than in front of a place of worship. Everywhere there were soldiers, some talking in groups, others walking about purposefully. They all wore thick leather jerkins and some the bright-coloured sashes and the wide-brimmed hats trimmed with fine plumes, that Danny recognised from pictures as the Royalist gear. So that was it, he was in the Royalist camp. He felt a tug on his sleeve and turned and saw the blonde-haired chap.

'Oh, there you are Erik,' said Danny, crossing his fingers that he'd got the right name. It was, because his new friend drew close to him and said:

'Aye it's me. I've been finding out what we're to be about today – we're to be taking stuff up to them on the roof.' Eric paused and then lowered his voice, drawing Danny a bit nearer to him. 'Daniel, I know you're a Bagot, but haven't you got the fear in you today?' Erik looked around, as if worried that some-one might overhear.

'Why should I have?'

'Oh that's just like someone from the Bagot family. What's to be frightened about? Well...there's only Lord Brooke – one of Parliament's best commanders with his soldiers – a thousand good fighting men out-side the gates, and as likely as not to be joined by more parliament soldiers from Derbyshire in a few days' time. They're all desperate to finish off this Royalist stronghold.'

'Yes I know,' said Danny (he didn't know at all, of course but he wanted to keep Erik talking so as to learn what was going on). 'But why is Lichfield so important to them?'

'You know full well, the Royalists use this city as a stopping place from the King's headquarters at Oxford on the way to the north-east ports. And any of us they can lay their hands on are not just going to be given a ticking off, are we?' He looked meaningfully at Danny and then drew his hand dramatically across his throat to indicate decapitation.

'You mean they might succeed in getting into the Close?'

'Well... now then' said Erik, with a nervous look over his shoulder. 'What sort of talk is that from a Bagot? Don't let your uncle hear or you'll be in for a whipping.' Then he said in a much louder voice for anyone who might have overheard their conversation: 'Them walls are so thick and the gates so strong, nobody will ever be able to breach them!' Danny was sure that Erik was really scared and that his sudden bluster was to keep his own spirits up, as well as to convince anyone listening he was a true Royalist supporter.

'Just as I said, Erik, there's nothing to be frightened about.' Danny wished for his new friend's sake, that could be true.

'We must get about our tasks' said Erik, leading the way through the crowds into the main doors of the cathedral.

Inside, there seemed to be hundreds of Royalist supporters, and anyone could see that what they were about, was preparation for battle. There were men cleaning guns, all sorts of bits of metal being scraped and polished; men and women filling little wooden tubes with powder (gunpowder thought Danny) and soldiers in flamboyant uniforms, sharpening the blades of their swords and daggers. Everywhere the more humble folk were carrying things: buckets of water, piles of wood, barrels and sacks with whatever in – was it food? There were few smiles on people's faces; most looked grimly determined. You could feel tension building. Danny spotted two men who seemed to be having a quarrel, their faces contorted with anger. The cathedral was no longer a place of worship – it was a soldiers' barracks. Danny noticed halfway down the nave on the north wall, a table with what looked like bandages, pots of ointment and some really gruesome-looking instruments. Those must be the surgeon's tools; it was a ghastly thought.

'See that blue flag over there leaning against that pillar in the nave. You'll be expected to carry that one – the Bagot's regiment of foot – if the ensign gets killed.'

'Oh,' said Danny, 'it won't come to that.'

'Don't be too sure. Think about what happened yesterday. And remember our colonels can't count on the townsfolk: their loyalties lie mostly with Parliament's men. So the best place for us supporters of the King, is to be here in the Close. But come on, we need to get up on the roof to see what's wanted by them up there.'

'What's wanted?' repeated Danny wondering how on earth they were going to get up on the roof. He hoped that it wasn't by going up ladders.

'We might need to start carrying up gunpowder and stuff.'

'Right, you lead the way Erik.'

'I will, but don't you go getting all spooky with me up the spiral staircase just cos it's dark.'

'I won't,' said Danny relieved to hear the word staircase but puzzled because he hadn't heard of such a thing in the present-day cathedral.

They made their way through to the south transept, to a small door set in the west wall near the main southern pilgrim door. It was very dark in the stairwell and as they climbed up the narrow, tightly-turning steps, Danny wondered if Erik's mention of being spooked, was because that's how he felt: Erik kept up a tuneless little whistle most of the way up – whistling in the dark, thought Danny. The steps seemed endless and there would be no possibility of passing anyone coming down. Fortunately, they didn't meet anyone. At last, a gleam of light! But, they were not quite at the top yet, there were a few more steps to climb before they were out on the roof. And then, relief – they were up. The view was breathtaking. They stood still, looking out at the spread of the town below, the jumble of rooftops and streets, and then the countryside stretching beyond with green fields, the slow wind of the river through the valley and the rise of hills in the distance.

'Wow!' thought Danny, clutching the top of a stone parapet, 'this is amazing.' The people below looked like the small inhabitants of toytown; even the enemy, camped so dangerously close on the other side of the moat, looked more like toy soldiers than the real thing.

'This is a really good view – you can see exactly what's going on,' Danny said.

'The first class shots are positioned up here,' whispered Erik, as if his words might drift down on the wind to be heard by the enemy below. 'I don't know many of them but you will recognise John Dyott.'

'Err... John Dyott?'

'Yes, you know 'Dumb Dyott.' He's related to Richard Dyott of Freeford Manor – he's called 'Dumb' because he can't speak.'

Danny suddenly remembered his mum telling him once that in the past, people who were deaf were often called 'deaf and dumb' because they didn't learn to speak when they were little, and people thought there was an actual condition where you couldn't speak, but in fact there was no such condition, it was just that they were deaf. Danny thought, he had better pretend he knew of Dumb Dyott, so he said:

'Oh yes, I've heard of John Dyott.' He wanted to explain to Erik that it would be nicer to use the man's christian name than call him 'Dumb', but this wasn't the time or place.

One important-looking soldier with a long well-groomed moustache and wearing a particularly bright sash across his shoulder came up to them and asked them to bring up some water, and then he warned:

'You lads be careful up here – there are the odd snipers taking shots already. They haven't got their aim in yet, but you can never be too careful and…' he started grinning, 'we don't want to lose our errand boys before they've done their work, now do we? Eh what do you say chaps? Two lads with missing heads will be no good to us will they?'

'They won't, Captain,' laughed a subordinate with thick, bushy red hair that looked as if at least a couple of birds were nesting in it. As he laughed, Danny caught sight of his black teeth.

'Have you lads had yer victuals?' asked the captain.

'No sir,' said Erik.

'Well, get something to eat and then bring the water up – it's going to be a busy day. Go on lads, get some food, for you'll be running up and down those steps like monkeys, fetching and carrying.'

'Yes, sir,' they answered in unison.

They crept down the steep, stone steps with hands on the walls to steady themselves, both thinking it was much easier coming down than going up.

'The only trouble is,' said Erik, 'we'll be carrying stuff going up and coming down empty-handed. I wish it was the other way round.'

'No good wishing,' said Danny. 'It looks as if we're in for a hard day.'

As they reached the bottom, Erik darted off towards the west door where bread, cheese and various flat cakes were piled high on a table. Danny thought that it wasn't that long since he'd had his tea, so he'd give the food a miss. He wandered down one of the aisles and was intrigued to see two clergymen wrapping up what he thought were probably cathedral treasures. He caught sight of a flash of gold and silver. Cups, plates and the altar cross were being hastily bundled into a huge wooden chest with metal banding, no doubt to be taken to a safe hiding place.

Suddenly, it seemed as if the cathedral went quiet, the noise was still there but muffled. Danny became aware of a presence: something, someone was there, and then the calm, kind face of the monk that he had seen on his visit to Lichfield in 671 appeared like a vision. The face was there in front of his eyes, as clear as he had seen it the first time. And then it faded. Now he strangely felt himself getting angry – angry with the idea of a battle going on in his beautiful building. Who were the Parliamentarians to lay siege to it? And who were the King's soldiers to use it as a garrison? It should belong to the people who needed it.

He was quickly jolted out of his strange mood by a soldier shouting:

'Out of me way lad,' as he struggled past with a barrel under each arm.

The man seemed angry like him, and put his barrels down, looking at Danny in a quizzical manner as if to ask him to solve a problem.

'Do you know what day it is today, boy?' asked the stranger.

'No sir'.

'It's the second of March, that's what it is. It's St. Chad's Day!'

'The day of St. Chad!' exclaimed Danny, a strange shiver going up his spine.

'Aye, but don't you worry lad,' said the stranger. 'Our patron saint is looking down on us now – he'll see to those threatening us at our gates – he'll protect us from Lord Brooke – I know it.'

Then he just walked on.

'Well,' thought Danny, 'I wasn't spooked on the dark stairs, but now I'm definitely spooked. I think I'd better find Erik.' Erik wasn't near the table with the food anymore. Then Danny spotted him near the west door. He had acquired two buckets, (they were pails to him).

'Here, take yer pail. We must fill them from the well.' Danny was not impressed. The pail was made of wood with a metal hoop round it and was heavy before any water was in it. They went outside to the well that was close to the cathedral walls. Fortunately, Erik seemed to think it was his job to wind the pails down into the well, perhaps because two girls were standing by, giggling and nudging each other.

'What strong lads we have here Betsy,' the prettiest one teased. This made Erik pick up the pail as if it was the lightest thing and march off with his shoulders back, while Danny struggled behind. The pail had a nasty rope handle that dug into your hand. It was a slog up the stairs, but they both went slowly, taking care not to spill any precious water. As Danny put one foot in front of the other up the dark stairway, the words: 'Do you know what day it is today, boy?' echoed in his mind.

This time, when they reached the roof, a barrage of noise came at them. The men on the roof were firing almost non-stop now; one man taking aim, another preparing the gun. The enemy below was returning the fire. The two lads poured the water into a round butt and soon several men were dipping their tankards in and patting the lads on the back, in gratitude for quenching their thirst. On the way back to the well, feeling blisters starting on his hands from the rough rope handle, Danny went and got a strip of material from the 'hospital' table and wound it round the rope. The pail was much easier to carry like that. Danny was glad that Erik, hurrying to get back to the well, didn't see what he did. Obviously Erik wasn't getting blisters; his hands were hardened from doing similar tasks in his every day life.

'Hey Erik, I think that girl we saw at the well fancied you.' Danny teased on the way back up.

'Oh, what makes yer say that?' Erik replied.

'Just the way she was looking at you.' Danny could tell Erik was mightily chuffed. 'She was...' he was going to say 'a looker' but realised Erik wouldn't understand that term so ended up lamely with... 'a pretty girl.'

'Oh, she's that all right, but there's many a one wants to catch Annie Hobson's eye. Do you think she was looking at me?'

'Oh definitely, Erik. I know these things.'

After another trip up, they were commanded to bring up the soldiers' victuals. Victuals were round, flat loaves of bread that Danny thought didn't seem too fresh and chunks of a strong-smelling cheese. They waited at the food table because a small, chubby man with an air of great importance, the cook, was sure it was his job to pack up the food for 'our brave lads on the roof.' He carefully picked out what he judged to be the best loaves and pieces of cheese and wrapped them in a cloth, tying the four corners together so none fell out.

'This'll keep em going until I get some heat in the fire to cook that mutton the farmers have brought in,' he said. He passed them a bundle each and then wagged a finger at them: 'No nibbling mind, on the way up.'

'Victuals here!' One soldier gave the shout as soon as Erik and Danny appeared on the roof. The sound of shooting stopped as men put down their guns and came round, bent double to keep themselves below the parapet. The sound of firing from below carried on. As the boys untied their bundles and spread the food on the floor, the soldiers grabbed handfuls and were soon stuffing bread and cheese into their mouths as quickly as they could. Danny had to stop himself staring, for he had never seen food eaten in such a way. The men had beards, moustaches or a day's stubble for those who might have shaved in the normal way and plenty of crumbs ended up stuck to whiskers. One of them came up to Danny and put a grimy hand on his shoulder:

'Here Bagot boy, come round this side and see the enemy.'

Danny followed the soldier. 'Keep yer head down below the parapet. Brookey's men are returning our fire with a vengeance now and some of their marksmen are not half bad.'

What Danny saw was alarming. There were a great many more soldiers now in the enemy camp.

'There's a lot more of them than there is of us in the Close,' whispered Danny.

'They don't look prepared well though, do they?' said the soldier.

'What do you mean?' asked Danny.

'Well', the soldier replied, 'they're not formed up in battle order.'

'Perhaps they realise that the walls are well-manned and the fabric of the walls too solid for them to breach easily,' offered Danny.

'Maybe,' said the soldier 'but it's early days: we have to prepare for a long siege. That's the top and bottom of it. It's a siege and they'll try to starve us out and pick us off one by one from the top here, because this roof up here is the one advantage we've got.' He paused for a moment, prepared his gun, took aim and fired. Danny saw an enemy soldier go down.

'You hit him!'

'Aye, I generally do. But if he's gone down, another one will take his place. We are the better marksmen, but they've got the numbers and a siege is the worst. We never like sieges because first the ammunition runs out ... then the food and then the water and then...', he paused, 'and then we begin to die from starvation and disease and the wounded die from their wounds, which sometimes go gangrenous, and then they scream for a priest and beg to have their lives ended.'

Danny was startled, shocked at the roughness in the man's voice.

'Just thought you should know, you and the other lads, what a battle is: it's death and more bloody death.'

Danny nodded. He didn't know what to say, but he needn't have worried because the marksman seemed to have forgotten about him. He was busy training his gun on the next unfortunate below.

Danny scuttled back towards Erik. He remembered the shield that SHARP said they had put around him. Would it really stop one of these bullets? He was not going to risk finding out, so he hunched up, keeping his head below the parapet. When he got back to Erik who was waiting at the top of the stairs for him, he asked:

'Erik, do you know what happens when wounds go gangrenous?'

'Ooh, that's really bad – the pain makes grown men cry like babbies. They scream for their mothers and shout to God to take them to heaven.'

'How does it start?' queried Danny.

'Oh, with wounds that go bad ways.'

Erik was peering out over the parapet, dangerously.

'Be careful Erik, the enemy are returning fire now,' Danny warned.

'Just look down there,' said Erik. 'Can you see that soldier carrying the flag?'

'You mean the purple one with a small St. George's Cross on a white background in the top left-hand corner?'

'Yes, that's Lord Brooke's regiment flag – Lord Brooke who's dead against our good lawful King Charles'

'How much do you know about Lord Brooke?' asked Danny as they started on their now very familiar way down the stairs.

'What do you mean, what do I know about Lord Brooke?'

'Well, is he a good man, kind to his wife and children?'

'Daniel Bagot, where do you get yer thoughts from? How would I be knowing that? He's supposed to be a very religious man and people say that he and his like, think they know better than the Church of England – they know better than our lawful King who rules by the Divine Right. But you know these things as well as I do.'

'I should do Erik; you're right but sometimes I forget it all because my head is too full of other things, like maybe the pretty Annie was looking at me, not you at all.'

'You – you snake in the grass!' exclaimed Erik.

'Just joking, just joking.'

They reached the bottom of the stairs and went for their next load to take up. This time it was to be gunpowder.

CHAPTER 11

The Hero of the Hour

Danny began to lose count of how many times he and Erik had been up and down the spiral stairway. Filling the buckets with water was still relatively safe, as the well was in a protected corner of the close, but now they were taking water for people in the main part of the cathedral as well. The situation here was starting to get grim. Injured men were being carried in. Some had wounds that could be treated: bound up with bandages to stop the flow of blood. Others, whom no one could help, lay on the rough bedding, their life ebbing away. Groans, muttered curses and stifled cries of pain could be heard above the general clatter. Sometimes a fearful scream of agony pierced the air and filled everyone with dread, as the surgeon extracted a bullet from the flesh of a leg, shoulder or arm. Danny and Erik took water to the wounded, dipping a wooden cup into their pail for them to drink from. Annie and Betsy were helping the women tying the bandages, their young hands now smeared with blood. There were no smiles on their faces now.

One time when Danny was on the roof, he over-heard the soldiers grumbling about their commander.

'Earl, or no Earl, the man's too old to be in charge – besides what does he know of battles?'

'Spent his life eating and drinking, that's what he's done.'

'Aye and that's why he canna climb the stairs – too rickety with the gout.' There was a short burst of laughter at this. The soldiers didn't care who heard them. Were they not risking their lives for the King?

'Maybe Prince Rupert will come to our aid.'

'Aye. A commander like that could turn this around.'

'Them lot down there've got Lord Brooke lead-ing them – no comparison. The man's got guts and knows what's needed to fight a battle. What have we got? The doddering old Earl of Chesterfied.'

Positioning himself carefully so as to be at an awkward angle for the marksmen below, one of the captains trained his spyglass to the south.

'Hell's teeth,' he called, 'it's him – it's Brookey – look, look there he is halfway down Dam Street, the doorway on the left. Can you see him?'

'By God! You're right.'

Danny moved to look. He spotted a helmeted

soldier. That must be Lord Brooke. The commander came from out of the shelter of a doorway, but then he stopped and looked up as if scanning the cathedral roof and, as he did so, a shot rang out, a shot from the central spire of the cathedral. It went straight through Lord Brooke's left eye and into his brain. Instant death! The feared commander lay dead in the street!

Danny was vaguely aware that Erik had jumped up and was heading for the stairs but in his mind came the words:

'St. Chad will protect us from Lord Brooke.'

When he got down the stairs, Danny could hear sounds of cheering. Erik had spread the news that Lord Brooke had been shot dead by a marksman on the central spire. Suddenly everyone felt hopeful – could it be that they might win through? People were slapping each other on the back and even the wounded seemed to be in less pain. Danny found himself almost rejoicing as well, as if he really was Daniel Bagot. He spotted Erik, holding forth to a little group about the scene on the roof that he had witnessed. The pretty Annie was standing beside him. As Danny went over, he could see that Erik was relishing a moment of glory with his pals.

'Did you see him fall?' asked Annie.

'I did,' fibbed Erik. 'He went straight down like a skittle.'

Danny gave him a grin and then a surprised look to wind him up. It hadn't been Erik that had actually seen the historic moment at all, but himself.

Everything seemed to quieten down for a while. It was obvious that the soldiers on the roof had been right about the Earl of Chesterfield. Despite this significant victory, the Earl did nothing to take advantage of the situation. Instead of quickly going on an offensive, to take advantage of any possible confusion in the enemy camp, he dithered and this gave Lord Brooke's second in command, a thoroughly unpleasant individual called Sir Edward Peyto, the time he needed. He was much feared and it didn't take him long to impress on those under him, that he was in charge and would not tolerate any weakness.

Enemy fire started to concentrate on the central spire of the cathedral where the shot had come from. Everyone knew who the marksman was, up there: it was John Dyott. How Dumb Dyott had managed such a shot from such a distance, was the talk and wonder of all. Now, when they went up on the roof, Erik and Danny were in much more danger. Bullets were coming not just from the direction of the enemy but were ricocheting off the stonework and could fly out in any direction. The Royalists, both on the roof and on the ground were desperately firing on the men installing a cannon at the South Gate. It was obviously why Lord Brooke had been in Dam Street.

A terrible rumour started to circulate. It concerned the women and children outside the protection of the cathedral. The rumour was that they were being rounded up by Parliamentarian soldiers. With a horrible certainty, Danny began to understand the words he had read in Dr Richardson's 'A Brief History of Lichfield Cathedral.'

'Edward Peyto commanding the Parliamentarians had given the order for his soldiers to hunt down the families, the wives and children of Royalist soldiers… Any household that appeared not to have a man in it was under suspicion and the women and children were rounded up and held captive.'

But they weren't just to be held captive. When he and Erik next went up on the roof, they could both see what was happening.

'It's the devil's work that Peyto's about,' swore one soldier putting his gun down. For there below them driven by the swords and pistols of Parliamentarian soldiers was a long row of women, some with babes in their arms. They walked slowly forward, hand-in-hand with small children, the full width of Dam Street. Danny could see that more and more women and children were being forced into the line of fire, six rows deep in all. Peyto had driven them out as a human shield to stop the Royalists on the ground firing. Everyone on the roof was so shocked, they forgot for the moment, to take care. Erik, incensed by what he saw, stood up to shake his fist at the enemy. Danny saw a marksman below take aim.

'Down, down, Erik,' he yelled, lunging towards his friend. As his hands grasped Erik's shoulders, a terrific bang exploded in Danny's ears, and a force rocked him and Erik backwards. Both of them landed on the floor of the walkway in a tangled heap, but unhurt. That, thought Danny, was the shield activating.

'Bagot, Daniel Bagot, yer saved me life!'

'Nah,' said Danny. 'I tripped.'

Danny wanted to say, that the most sophisticated protection shield ever devised had saved both of them. He knew that without a shadow of doubt either he or Erik would have been hit, maybe killed, by that bullet without the shield that SHARP had somehow constructed around him, which for a brief moment he had been able to share with Erik.

'The bullet must have passed within an inch of me. I've never heard a sound like it,' gasped Erik.

'No, nor have I.'

They crawled away to the stairway. Now the dark, narrow, spiralling steps seemed like a safe haven between the battle zone of the roof and the mayhem on the floor of the cathedral. Neither wanted to get to the bottom of the stairs anymore. There was a stench in the air, the stench of blood, guts and too many humans suffering. When they were down, a woman came up to Danny and asked if she could have his shirt for bandages. He pulled it off immediately and handed it to her.

'Do you want my socks?' She nodded. He passed them to her. Then realised that his mobile had been pulsing for a while. He looked round for Erik. He saw him sitting on a bench, head in hands.

'You've had enough haven't you, Erik?'

'Aye, thank goodness it will be nightfall soon.'

'Yes, you'll get a bit of peace then.'

'But what will tomorrow bring?'

'I don't know, I wish I did, Erik, I wish I did.' Danny walked away, back towards the stairwell. What he wanted to know was whether Erik and all the others he had met would survive this battle and live to tell

the tale. As he climbed the stairs he counted them.
When he got to number fifteen, the first two numbers
he needed to dial, he keyed in 15798, pressed the red
button and heard the strange whine seeming to whistle down the stairs towards him, then...Nothing.

CHAPTER 12

Pay Back Time

'Back in the bathroom!' He said out loud, with more relief than he thought it would ever be possible to feel.

'I'm back in our bathroom, Langdale Gardens, Bisley, Nottinghamshire 2010!'

Was this how the men back from the first flight to the moon felt when they splashed down in the Pacific? He looked in the mirror. He was really mucky, covered in grime and dust from the gunpowder. On his left arm there was a smear of dried blood. 'I bet I smell', he thought. He switched the shower on full blast and stepped under the gush of warm water and washed until every speck of dirt had swizzled down the plug-hole.

He dried quickly, worrying that the family would soon be back. He didn't need to worry; they were not back for another hour and a half. Time for him to put the breeches back in the space/time travel bag and tuck it on the shelf, unseen behind the money-box, put his pyjamas on and climb into bed. He was whacked out.

He couldn't keep his eyes open.

He woke with a start when the front door banged shut. He could hear them excitedly talking about the evening's events. Quickly trying to bring his senses together, Danny grabbed his DS, switched it on and sat up in bed, just as Jenny burst into his room.

'What are you doing in bed?' she asked.

'I tink I'b got a bit of cold.' Danny said, applying a huge handful of tissues to his nose. 'Griff was sneezing all ober be today.'

'Well I don't want it.' Jenny hastily backed out the room. 'I'm getting my new trainers.'

'I knew you would.'

'You'll have to get me a Snickers bar, Danny.'

'Got it already – look it's there on my computer desk.'

Jenny dodged into the room and grabbed the bar, calling out; 'Thanks Danny you're sooooo good to me.'

Later on he heard his mum on the stairs and he repeated his tissues-to-the-nose routine. She had come up with a cup of hot lemon and honey, and Danny was happy to see, a sandwich. He was so hungry.

'Any chance of anoder sandwich?'

'Well I suppose they say 'feed a cold starve a fever'. Obviously you've only got a cold, not a fever, thank goodness.' Danny saw the small cloud of worry disappear from his mother's face, and felt the nasty nag of guilt about deceiving his parents so much, tug at him.

A few days later when his 'cold' had gone or, to be more precise, when the palms of his hands weren't so red and blistered, Danny came down just before it was bedtime to talk to his mum. She was working as usual at her computer in her small office space under the stairs. Every evening now she was on the internet, researching information for the Higgins family tree. It had all started when two of the women at the health centre where Mrs Higgins worked had started on theirs. There was now quite some rivalry between the three of them as to how far back in time they could trace their ancestors. Mrs Higgins felt that, with her first class honours degree in history, she should be out in front. She was, by far, the most knowledgeable of the three, but because of her generous nature she was always helping her colleagues and this didn't help her position in the race.

'How's it going, Mum?' Danny asked, pulling up a chair to sit beside her at the computer.

'Not too badly, Danny, but I have got a bit stuck on the Higgins side. I don't seem to be able to go much further than 1703.'

'You've done really well to get that far back.'

'Well Doreen at work has got much further on her mother's side. But then they were quite a wealthy family. Did you want something?'

'Not exactly: there was something I wanted to tell you.'

Danny had brought 'A Brief History of Lichfield Cathedral' with him and he put it down in front of his mum.

'You know Mum, how I've never really understood you and Dad being so against war...' he paused.

His mum stopped peering at the computer screen and turned to look at him.

'Mmm Danny?'

'Well, this book Dr Richardson has given me about Lichfield has really changed my mind. I can see where you and Dad are coming from. War does terrible things to people.'

'You're right, Danny. It does and I'm so glad you can see that now. I always knew you would come to understand that; but I am puzzled.'

'Why?'

'Well, you've seen terrible things on the television; bombs destroying cities, civilians caught up in fighting, children maimed and injured – Afghanistan, Iraq, Palestine, Bosnia. You've learnt about the Second World War at school and seen documentaries of the trenches in the First World War. That didn't seem to change your mind.'

'None of it ever seemed real.' Danny said quietly.

'And this little book here, brought it to life for you did it?' Mrs Higgins picked the book up and turned it over. 'It doesn't even look very well written; I mean historically correct but hardly inspirational. I'll have to read it.'

Danny was feeling distinctly uncomfortable now. He had wanted somehow or other to make it up to his mum and dad for leading his double life, but it didn't seem to be working too well. Then his mum smiled at him.

'But Danny, it doesn't really matter what changed your mind; the important thing is you've changed your mind, and I'm so glad.' She gave him a hug. It was a quick, awkward hug, unlike Aunt Mabel, Rachel Higgins was not very good at hugs. Danny gave her a big hug back, and saw the look of surprise, but pleasure on his mum's face.

'Do you want to read this book, Mum?' He held up the Lichfield history.

'Definitely, Danny.'

'Well, I am going to be using it for the history topic that that new teacher Mr. Donnelly's asked us to do over the summer holidays, but I won't need it for a while.'

'What are you doing for your topic?'

'The civil war.'

'A bit of a big subject.'

'That's what Mr. Donnelly said so I am narrowing it down to the war up to the beheading of Charles the First.'

'He sounds OK, this new chap… Mr. Donnelly, did you say?'

'Yes. He's great. He's stopped the class clown, Wayne Haskins from mucking about. Nobody knows how he did it, but the rumour is he fixed him up with a job at the paper shop – you know the Haskins have absolutely no money.'

'That's no reason to look down on someone, Danny.'

'I wasn't. It's just that Wayne can be so irritating. He thinks it's funny to fall off your chair – I mean I stopped thinking that funny when I was about five.'

'Yes, well you're right, of course. Though I suppose the poor lad was doing it for a reason.'

'Anyway, the thing is he doesn't mess about any more and it seems to be down to Mr. Donnelly. The other thing was, Mum, when I said I was going to do my history topic on the civil war he said 'which one?'

'Oh clever chap. Sounds as if he knows what he's talking about.'

'He said there was one in the twelfth century between someone called Maud and King Stephen.

'That is quite correct.'

I'm going up to bed now Mum,' Danny stood up and pains shot up his legs. He'd suffered with stiff joints and painful calf muscles ever since his return from Lichfield 1643.

'Ooo..ouch,' escaped his lips before he could stop himself.

'What's the matter?' his mum asked.

'Oh I'm just stiff from the extra athletics training that I'm doing with Mark and Griff after school.'

'Danny, you mustn't do too much, you know that.'

'I'm fine, mum. You know how I like to get in shape for the track events. I've just left it a bit late this year, that's all.'

Danny was amazed how easily telling lies came to him. In fact, he had been doing no training at all. He had told his friends that because of his earlier hospital stay, he had to wait until the doctor gave him the all clear. In actual fact, he had no intention of missing the athletics that summer; he just wanted the stiffness from climbing hundreds of stone steps to wear off before he started running.

For the next week or two, Danny made a point of going down to see how his mum was doing with her research into the family tree. Things had certainly slowed down with the Higgins branch, in fact they seem to have come to a full stop, so she was now researching the Fletcher's a branch of her own family. Then one evening when Jenny had joined them, she said, never mind about the family tree stuff:

'Guess what I've found out from your little book 'A Brief History of Lichfield Cathedral'?'

'I've no idea, Mum,' said Danny.

'Well, how far have you got with your study of the civil war? Have you found out that the cathedral at Lichfield was besieged?'

'Oh, yes, I've written about that. The cathedral was the stronghold of the Royalists and the Parliamentarians, led by Lord Brooke, set up camp around the city, trying to breach the gates. They seriously outnumbered the Royalists, but a sharp shooter from one of the cathedral towers spotted Lord Brooke and shot him; it was the most amazing shot.'

'Wow Danny! Have you been up all night finding out all that stuff? Your teacher's going to be pleased.'

'Well, I'm very pleased,' said Mrs Higgins. 'You've worked very hard to get so much detailed information, Danny. As I've said, it's the detail in history that makes it interesting. But here is what I was about to tell you: the precious and ancient Gospel of St. Chad was kept in the cathedral at that time. It could have been destroyed if the Parliamentarians had got their hands on it, but it was whisked away to a place of safety by the precentor. You know that's the chap in charge of all the cathedral music, services and documents.'

'Like Dr Richardson?' put in Jenny.

'Well sort of, I suppose,' Mrs Higgins didn't want to waste time on explaining the exact difference; she wanted to get to the important bit of her story. 'What the book says is that the precentor at the time was called William Higgins!'

'Hurray – a famous, a noble, a brave ancestor!' shouted Jenny.

'Hey, calm down,' said Mrs Higgins. 'We've no

proof of that.'

'But it could be, Mum,' said Danny.

'Yes, I suppose it could be.'

'You're sure to find a link, Mum,' said Jenny. 'Just fancy an ancestor of ours saving the precious St. Chad Gospel.'

'Two Higgins's in the cathedral,' Danny said, so quietly that the other two, peering now at the computer screen did not hear properly but Jenny glanced up at him and saw that strange 'out of it' look that she had come to recognise so often on her brother's face.

'You know, Mum, how Danny's changed so much. He used to be easy to understand but now he is so different. I mean, he used to hate history and now he spends all his time researching historical facts; he's writing a book that we never get to read and he's happy to keep his old mobile, even though you and Dad offered to get him a new one for his birthday. He's a boy of 'mystery' and I think he's leading a double life. I think M15 have recruited him for a spy.'

'Oh Jenny,' laughed Mrs H. 'You do talk nonsense – time for me to start on the tea. Out of my way you two. I'm doing pasta bake tonight. How about that? Oh, and by the way, we've got to watch that dreadful lottery programme later on; I won the weekly raffle at work today: the five lottery tickets. We might be lucky and win a ten pound prize with one of them.'

Danny felt a tingle go down his spine. His mum always bought the weekly raffle ticket at the health centre where she worked, the prize for which consisted of five lottery tickets. In all the years she had worked there, she had never won the weekly raffle and so never had a chance at the lottery. Dad would not buy a lottery ticket on principle. Could it be that the promise Professor Aurelia Dobbs had made was about to be kept?

That night, one of the lottery tickets that Mrs Higgins had laid out on the lounge coffee table won a prize of five thousand pounds. The Higgins's longed-for extension, and for which they had been saving madly for two years, was now a possibility.

COMPETITIONS AND ACTIVITIES

Seven Arches Publishing often runs competitions for you to enter with prizes of book tokens, that can be spent in any bookshop, for solving puzzles or for a good illustration. Why not go to www.sevenarches-publishing.co.uk and check out whether there is competition or activity on its way based on one or other of our books. We often include the winning entries of our competitions, or the writing, poems or pictures that you send us in the next print run of the title.

PUBLISHING WITH PRINCIPLES

Our books for children are not only exciting adventures, they stretch and challenge them as readers and learners, and are unlikely to pander to the latest trends. Our first book, 'Nidae's Promise' encouraged wonder at the amazing life of swallows. Danny Higgins – Time Traveller, the first in our series 'The Time-Travelling Kids' celebrates the history of our nation.

We are striving to make our business a good place for people to work and to offer employment to those, who through disabilities or other reasons, have found it difficult to get work elsewhere.

Our books are printed in this country so that delivery is nearby and the paper used is from managed forests.

CONTACT US

You are welcome to contact Seven Arches Publishing by:
Phone: 0161 612 0866
Or
Email: admin@sevenarchespublishing.co.uk

PLACES TO VISIT TO FIND OUT MORE ABOUT LICHFIELD AND THE SURROUNDING AREA

Lichfield Cathedral: Open to visitors every day except during special services.

Phone: 01543 306100

The Heritage Centre: St Mary's, Market Square, Lichfield.

Phone: 01543 256611

Drayton Manor Theme Park: A fun day out for all the family.

Collect the other books in the Time Traveller Kids series

When a mysterious boy claiming to be from a future organisation called SHARP contacts him on his mobile, Danny agrees to travel back in time to the Tudor period.

Danny's interest in history is zero, but somehow making friends in the long forgotten past gets him seriously hooked on time travel.

Incredibly musically gifted, Atlanta is entranced by the music of the far-into-the- future humankind. Is this what makes her agree to join the growing band of twenty first century kids who go back in time to gather information, for the organisation called SHARP?

To be published November 2010.

When Alex McLean is catapulted back to 1314 by a rival outfit to SHARP, his life is in serious danger. They do not care if he falls to his death with the desperate band of Scots fighters who did the impossible and scaled the terrifying Rock on which Edinburgh Castle stands to this day.